Carol-Anne was born in Fife, Scotland, before moving to the Midlands, when she was seven years old and to Cheshire when she was fifteen. It was a story told to her as a child that inspired her writing. Carol-Anne met her husband in Cheshire in 2012; they married in 2013 and three years later, Carol-Anne graduated from Staffordshire University with a PGCE in Primary Education. Having previously worked with younger children, Carol-Anne has a love for learning and loves to see the children in her care develop and grow. She now lives in Lancashire with her husband and their son. They enjoy family days out and have recently discovered their enjoyment for family cruises.

For Seth – this story grew as you did – you are both, precious and beautiful to me.
And to Dom, you believed in me and made me whole.

For all my family and friends who knew and encouraged me – thank you!

C. N. Naylor

MEMOIRS OF FAERIES

Taha,

Be awesome!

x

AUSTIN MACAULEY PUBLISHERS™

LONDON · CAMBRIDGE · NEW YORK · SHARJAH

A CIP catalogue record for this title is available from the British Library.

ISBN 9781528925983 (Paperback)
ISBN 9781528964524 (ePub e-book)

www.austinmacauley.com

First Published (2019)
Austin Macauley Publishers Ltd
25 Canada Square
Canary Wharf
London
E14 5LQ

I would like to begin by thanking my parents; they helped me to believe that I could achieve anything I put my mind to. The rich and colourful childhood experiences that they provided my siblings and me, sparked my imagination and creativity from a young age.

Secondly, I would like to thank my older brother Ross – one of the most talented beings I know – I asked if he would illustrate my book and he agreed instantly. I am very proud to have written the first book that he will have illustrated.

To the long list of unpaid reviewers and editors that are my friends, thank you for taking the time to read and comment on my writing – even with the heaps of marking that teachers already have!

Dom, you kept me going even when the pregnancy hormones made me tired. I would not have finished this book if it wasn't for your continuous support and love.

And finally, to my readers, here is a little insight into the mind of a creative, fun-loving little girl. I hope that you enjoy reading this as much as I enjoyed writing it.

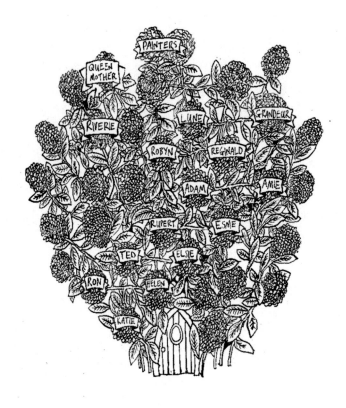

Faerie n, (pl. faeries): a magical being, diminutive in size and considered to be imaginary by humankind.

Chest heaving, I sped on. I was running out of time. They would find out if I didn't get back. How on earth would I explain this one? I couldn't. No, stop thinking like that. I wouldn't have to. I ran faster, jumping over rocks and brambles; ducking through the undergrowth and dodging stalks of overgrown grass. I could see the sun, low in the sky as I pressed on, lungs bursting and heart hammering inside my chest to the point where it actually hurt. I sank my bare toes into the soft earth and pushed on faster, using my arms to propel me further and faster forward.

Then – there it was. The door, my escape. It was almost over. I pulled it open, slipped through and slammed it shut. I sank down to the ground with my back to the door and closed my eyes. I counted, in my head, to ten. 1...2...3...4. My breathing started to calm. I felt my legs stretch out in the dirt. 5...6...7. My hair snagged in the bushes above me now. 8...9...I opened my eyes...10. Through the slats of the garden fence, I could see that the sun was just beginning to set. My breathing back to normal, I stood up and walked around the trunk of the tree; my eyes met hers. I froze. Wide-eyed and cheeks glistening with tears sat my daughter, Helen. Clutching her rag doll to her chest, she looked up at me.

"You were gone, Mummy," she cried. "I looked everywhere for you."

Panicking, I picked her up, she was cold and shivering; I held her close and wrapped my arms tightly around her. As much as I wanted to share all of this with her, she mustn't know. She was much too young and wouldn't be able to keep such a big secret.

"Aw hunny, don't cry," I soothed, "Mummy is just very good at hide and seek." I hoped that would fix things for now.

9

I kissed her forehead and wiped away her tears with the back of my hand.

As we walked back to the house, I scolded myself. How could I have been so careless to allow time to get so late? Didn't I know, didn't I understand what could happen? Of course I did – but I had needed to get away and then, inside, I had been having such a good time... classic 'Cinderella-at-the-ball' syndrome.

Did you ever know that at the bottom of your garden, between the rhododendrons and hydrangeas, underneath the lowest bows and between the twigs and rocks, there exists – only to those who believe – a small door to a world beyond your imagination?

Always believe Katie, and it will be.

Part One

Before

Chapter One
Katie

Always believe Katie, and it will be.

These were a few of the last words that I remember my grandmother telling me when I was about seven years old.

Growing up, she had told me the most wonderful stories. I would ask her whenever I saw her to tell me a tale about her childhood – and she would – but interwoven into every tale was magic, real magic. I loved magic – maybe because my grandma told me about it with such passion in her voice and in her eyes and with such clarity and detail; there wasn't a question she couldn't answer. She made it all sound so real. She would tell me stories about faeries and the faerie world. About how she had visited it, been on adventures and even met the Queen. How she had ridden on the back of a bumblebee, a butterfly and migrated to warmer countries on the back of birds. Her tales told of the times she had travelled the world using magic and faerie dust and as a young child, who could fathom the magic of such things; I loved it and believed every word. There was not a doubt in my mind that, at the bottom of Grandma's garden, there was a faerie door to a magical kingdom. At four, five, six and seven years old, I was young and my imagination was fierce enough to allow me to believe in magic.

My grandma had died when I was eight and I think, looking back at how my life changed, some of the magic died with her. Alzheimer's is a cruel disease that steals the memories and personality of a person – I don't remember much of my grandma once she became ill, as my mother and father kept me away for my own sake. But I heard them speak of her and the words they spoke about this lady made her sound less and less like the Grandma that I had known. I missed her. I missed her magical fairy-tales and so whenever I had chance after her death, I would take myself away and visit the bottom of her garden; crouch down on my heels, dress dragging in the dirt and peer under the bushes for the door. The door that Grandma spoke of. I sometimes would speak out to the faeries.

"Hello? Hello? My grandma said that there were faeries who lived here… Hello? Please, can I see you? Can I see the door and come in?" I whispered intently in my politest voice.

I didn't find any door. Unbeknown to me, the absence of her tales and the nearing of my teenage years was slowly stripping me of my childhood innocence and ability to believe. As I grew up, I began to lose the magic. Eventually, I stopped believing. Or rather, I didn't have cause to – I found new things to dream of: ponies, dresses, friends (who did not believe in magic) and certainly not faeries at the bottom of the garden.

School was hard work. I was nine and a half years old and in year five at the local primary school; like most children in my class, I found maths complicated, I didn't understand the questions that I was asked when we did reading and had the messiest handwriting – which drove my teacher mad.

"Katie," she'd say to me at the end of the day, "you need to redo this piece of work at playtime tomorrow; it simply isn't neat enough."

It was, sadly, not an uncommon occurrence for me to spend my playtimes rewriting my English, science or history work. I didn't mind too much, especially in the winter. I would kick off my shoes and warm my toes on the heating pipes that ran around the perimeter of the room. I'm not sure that my work was ever neater at the end of the playtime – my writing was never going to change regardless of how much extra handwriting work was sent home or however many hours Mum and Dad would sit and try to get me to form my letters correctly. As soon as my pencil hit the page, it had a mind of its own. My brain also worked much quicker than my writing could cope with. I was creative and I wanted to get as many of my ideas onto the page as I could. I loved to write and the quality was good. My teacher told my parents that at parent's evening – it was just rushed and messy.

During one such playtime, in year five, as the warmth of the hot water in the pipes spread through my feet and up my legs, my hands loosely gripping the pen as I wrote, my mind began to wander. It wandered back to my grandma and her stories, her colourful and vibrant tales of magic and faeries. I was always daydreaming. If my grandma had still been alive, she would have taken full credit for that! I was (as would become apparent to me in due course) very like her in many, many ways. My mind flooded with memories as I allowed it to pursue moments and emotions from long ago, both my memories and her tales began to spring to life inside my head.

"Katie!" I awoke abruptly. "Katie, have you finished your work yet? Playtime is almost over and you are daydreaming! Get on with it before the others come back in." And so I did, dutifully, copy the words out once again in my book. Would my teacher ever realise that this was not making any difference? I just had messy writing and that was that.

The first time I stayed over at Grandma and Grandad's house was when Mum and Dad went on a skiing holiday. They loved their holidays in the Alps; skiing and staying in log cabins – drinking wine and enjoying the crackling heat from the open fire by night and experiencing the thrill of the cold, bright slopes by day. I was five years old at the time and deciding that this would be their last skiing holiday until I was much older, they left me in the care of my grandparents. The next holiday would be one that I would enjoy too. Most children would moan about having to stay with 'old people' but I loved it! Grandpa's office was filled floor to ceiling with books, with stacks of books decorating the corners too. You could smell the age of the paper and the yellowing of the pages inside the books that I pulled off the shelf gave me goose bumps. My mum, Helen, loves books too – whenever we pass a second-hand bookshop, she has to go in. I once saw her flick through the pages of a book with her thumb and inhale the smell of the books. She liked to make up a story about every book and got even more excited if someone had written in the margin or underlined some of the text. I certainly got my love of books from her, and she got hers from my grandad. Every book you could imagine filled this room. Quite often, when I inevitably woke up earlier than them both, I would tiptoe downstairs and sit in the office imagining that this was my library. I would sniff the air like my mum and pull books off the shelf willy-nilly even if I could not read them and pretend. To the smaller than average five-year-old that I was, an average-sized room filled to the rafters with books seemed so huge.

I loved books. But there was one book that I longed for, it sat about three quarters of the way up, it was a beautifully bound leather book with a length of thin leather holding it closed. It was always just out of my grasp. Yet even from my eye level, it looked magical and I yearned to reach it.

On other occasions, I would do the gardening with Grandma. This was just as much fun. She was a keen gardener, she knew everything about everything; the names of all the plants and what colours the flowers would be and the name of every garden bird. She would lovingly tend to the flowers, cut back the hedges and pull up the weeds. There was a beautifully ornate sundial in her garden and she taught me how to tell the time from it.

"In bright sunshine the sundial casts a clear shadow," she would explain again once I was old enough to understand. "It is this shadow that shows the time," pointing to the position of the shaded part of the dial and the number that was being pointed to. "Only the idea of using the sun to find the time is not as familiar as it used to be," she spoke as though there were years and years of experience in them. I could listen to my grandma all day, every day.

In the garden, there were bird feeders, a bird bath and a bird table which was always laden with treats. Very often, we would use leftover scraps of food and make fat balls for the birds and hang them up after they had gone solid. Then we would sit and watch the birds feast on them from behind the patio doors. Every visit to my grandparents' house was special. Sometimes, I would sit in Grandpa's lap and he would read to me from whatever book I chose from the shelf of children's books. Sometimes old fables, other times adventure stories about elves and dwarves and dragons, stories about quests and battles. If I was lucky enough, sometimes he would ask me to create the main characters and items from the story and he would concoct his own magical tale of wonder just for me. These were very special occasions for me and sometimes I wondered if my grandpa had been touched by magic as well as Grandma.

In the house, every ornament had a story and, at bedtime, I would snuggle deep down into the eiderdown bedding with the patchwork quilt pulled up to my chin and my head sinking into the feather down pillow, I would ask for more stories. Even the memories gave me goose bumps.

My daydreams were often filled with images from her wonderfully creative stories. I would imagine that I was there with her and it filled me with joy and excitement. Yet, afraid that others would find them childish, I never shared them with my friends for I was old enough now to feel self-conscious about what others might think, I was afraid of being laughed at, excluded from their group or talked about negatively. It was all too common an occurrence between the girls and boys in school. You would often hear tales of 'weird' children and, sadly, bullying is not something that a child can easily avoid once it has started. I resolved to keep Grandma's stories to myself and to save myself from anything untoward.

On one occasion, I dreamt of a faerie world where my Grandma was the Queen. She floated, perfectly balanced and oh-so-elegant on one of the flyaway seeds of a dandelion clock. I smiled as my thoughts raced back over previous years. This one was a recurring daydream, nothing changed ever – from one lucid moment to the next, regardless of whether I was dreaming by day or dreaming by night. It was almost as if it was a memory and not just a story that my mind played and replayed over and over again. It was so vivid, so colourful

– there was too much attention to detail for my childish mind to have created; the veins in each leaf that I saw, the grains of sand under my feet, the rainbow hues in the wings of the fairies and the way the sunlight shimmered through their translucency.

I came to after one daydreaming session feeling emotional and this was confusing for a child of nine years old. I couldn't fathom it, nor could I talk about it with my friends. I wondered if my mum would think I was making up stories if I told her – so I resolved not to.

It was later that evening, I remember the date, almost the summer holidays – July 7th – as I was eating dinner with my mum and dad that I brought up Grandma. We talked about her from time to time but never for long; Mum got easily upset, her eyes would glass over and Dad would change the subject. My mum missed her mum. Even more so since Grandpa had moved out of the old family home and into an old people's home. I think she felt as though she had lost both her parents.

Grandpa might have moved into an old persons' residential home but he was still totally sane, would talk for hours about government and politics. I didn't understand a word of it, but he would tirelessly explain each politician's viewpoint and I, being the devoted child that I was, would listen intently and try to remember every word that he spoke. Long gone were the stories and magical tales, left behind in the house, gone with Grandma. Maybe it made his heart ache to tell the kinds of stories that she had told and lived and loved. He watched the news everyday (and for as long as the other residents would allow him to). Glasses perched on the end of his short nose, eyebrows grey and sticking out at odd angles, thinning grey hair combed neatly to the left and blue, bright blue, eyes twinkling as he smiled. Grandpa was in a wheelchair now; he had lost his leg below the knee when he was a soldier and as he had grown old, he had lacked strength in his good leg meaning that he struggled to stand. And then his upper body strength lessened so that he was no longer able to use his crutches. I think, behind his smile, he missed Grandma too and he still had her photograph at the side of his bed and Mum told me that he still kissed her goodnight before bed.

Back at the dinner table, I spoke, breaking the silence.

"I thought about Grandma today."

Dad looked at me and then at Mum, who smiled.

"Did you, dearest?" she replied, probably squeezing Dad's hand under the table to let him know that she was alright. "What did you think?"

"Well, it was just for a moment." I smiled, remembering. "I was thinking about her stories – the ones she would tell me at bedtime."

"Oh, she was a story-teller alright!" Dad chuckled. "She once told me how she had flown on a dandelion seed!" He closed his eyes for a moment before adding, "And a butterfly – so convincing was she that I would often pinch myself to check I wasn't dreaming. Her stories were so magical and the way she told them…"

I looked at Mum, her eyes were glassy again and I wondered if I should change the subject, but she was smiling so I asked, "Did she tell you stories too, Mum?"

"She certainly did. Lots of wonderful stories, Katie; about animals, woodland fairies and birds. Your grandmother loved nature, she knew every garden bird, almost by name and every flower, what it smelt like and what colours it could be."

We sat quietly for a moment before Mum suggested that I brush my teeth, run my bath and get ready for bed. My bedtime routine was fixed. It had been ever since I could remember. Teeth, bath, bed, story and sleep. Every night.

Mum brushed my hair and kissed my forehead before she tucked me into bed and headed for the door. She paused and looked over her shoulder, "I'm glad you remember Grandma," she breathed, "She was a very special lady. Good night, sweetheart."

"Goodnight, Mum."

She closed the door, and I drifted peacefully off to sleep.

Chapter Two
Helen

Watching my daughter sleep is like nothing else in the world. My child, my miracle; my whole life revolved around caring for and loving this little girl. She was so like me in so many ways. I loved her vivacity for life. I sat with my back against the bannisters at the top of the stairs and watched her through the half-closed door. She was everything and more than a mother could hope for. And yet, I suppose, like most mothers I'm sure – there was a niggle, a doubt, a worry, that something would go wrong, that she would not have the life that I dreamt for her. Still, this feeling wasn't new to me and so, like always, I pushed it to the back of my mind, tucked my feet underneath me and pushed myself up to standing. I took one last look at Katie, she was cocooned in her quilt, her teddy bears and dolls surrounding her. She looked so beautiful.

I visited my dad at the care home a couple of days later. I wish I had time to see more of him. Sitting opposite him, I really had to question why a man who still had full control of his incredible mind had to live in a care home. I felt like the worst daughter. He was drinking his cup of tea and reading the newspaper.

"So how is my Katie?" he asked as he lifted his eyes above the top of the broadsheet, looking over the top of the glasses that perched on his nose.

"She's good, thanks, Dad. She is doing well at school, except she has the messiest handwriting and still misses most playtimes to redo her work – but I don't think it bothers her!"

"Messy handwriting signifies a great mind," he mumbled as he went back to reading his paper. "Just like my Elsie."

I loved hearing my dad call my mum that – they had been so close and so in love. Yet to know them, you wouldn't have put them together in a million years! Dad was so sensible and Mum had been so eccentric and had had such flair. They must have kept each other on their toes!

"How are you finding it in here, Dad?" I asked.

He paused, put down his paper and looked at me in the eye. "Listen, Helen, I am fine. Stop fretting over me." He knew me so well. I did fret, I felt guilt like I had betrayed him. "It was the best thing, love," he continued. "I couldn't manage that big house by myself. I couldn't manage the stairs or get to the upstairs loo and sleeping in the lounge... well your mother wouldn't have liked that. Who sleeps in the lounge!?" He laughed and his eyes twinkled.

"I just don't like to see you here – you don't fit in. Half these people have lost their minds and don't know what day it is! You are still following politics!"

"Helen." He took a breath and then started, "In here, I don't have to cook, clean, make the bed, hoover, clean the toilet, do the ironing... Honestly, love. It suits me fine – what with my leg and not having your mum around." He looked at me, knowing what I wanted to say, that I could do those for him. "I know what is going around inside that head and I will not have my daughter doing my housework for me – you have your own house and family to care and provide for." With that, he lifted up his paper in mock indignation and carried on reading.

"There has been no interest in the house, Dad," I changed the subject. The house had been on the market for the last five months. He set his paper aside again.

"I have been thinking about that." His eyes twinkled as he continued, "that house was my grandfather's house and I wish there was a way we could keep it in the family. It doesn't need anything doing to it, it's ready to be moved straight into; there is no mortgage left on it and I have my savings to pay for this place. In fact, there is more than enough to keep me in here. I was very good at saving money all my life and since your mum left us, well, I haven't had anyone to spend it on." He looked at me, "I want you and Ron and Katie to have the house. You could keep yours and rent it or sell it to have a rainy day pot. But I really want you to have the house. The walls are full of our memories."

I was taken aback. I hadn't considered keeping the house – even when the thought of selling it had broken my heart. Dad saw my hesitation.

"Don't decide now – talk to Ron and Katie and then decide."

I stayed for another hour, listening to Dad talk politics and how history was repeating itself. Just before I left he said, "Remember – that house belongs to our family, Helen."

I kissed his forehead and said goodbye.

Chapter Three
Katie

Grandpa got his wish.

Four weeks later, on August 11th (the day after my tenth birthday), we had boxed up our house and possessions and were stood on the doorstep of our new house, with the removal lorry pulling up, full of boxes and furniture. Grandma and Grandpa's old house, Number 13, Thornbell Fold, Greater Whitherington was now our new home. Mum, Dad and I had discussed it the very night that Grandpa had suggested it and I had been both delighted and excited; Mum had shared in the enthusiasm and Dad had joined in with all the reasons why it would work.

"Oh please, Mum, please!" I had begged.

"I think I quite like the idea," piped up Dad, "it would be closer to work and there are good bus links for high school for Katie." He winked at me.

"I do think it's a wonderful idea, Mum had mused, but don't you think that it's a bit greedy of us?" She looked around the table at us. "I mean, we don't have to pay a penny for it and we will be renting this one and making money from it."

"It's what your dad wants, love," Dad spoke gently.

"I really, really want to, Mum," I had almost moaned. Mum and Dad smiled at me. The discussion had continued and the decision was made within an hour.

We spent the next few days moving furniture about, deciding what to keep, what to take and what to leave in this house as well as what would go where in the new house which had more rooms than ours had.

"Why are we calling it the new house when it is hundreds of years old?" I asked, puzzled. It was true, this house was made of stone and was at least 100 years old.

"Because it is new to us, our new home," Dad quipped with a grin.

"But it's actually Mum's old house too," I reminded him.

"Yep. It is," joined in Mum, "but it's going to be quite different now from when I lived here last, so I like the idea of it being a new adventure." She was frowning when she spoke but that frown became a smile after a second or so.

Once inside, I was allowed to choose from two bedrooms which I would like and once that decision was made, my bed and toy boxes were unloaded from the lorry, and the men who were helping us to move brought it all upstairs. It was my job to organise my clothes and toys into the wardrobe and cupboards.

I had chosen the bedroom that I had stayed in as a child; it overlooked the garden, which looked quite sad as it had gotten rather overgrown in the months since Grandpa had moved out. In fact, it was possibly longer than that since anyone had pruned the hedges or mown the lawn. Owing to the fact that Grandpa had been too weak to walk with his leg and crutches, I doubted that he would have been able to tend to the garden at all.

In the corner of the garden, I could see that the sundial was still there but was almost hidden by the hedges – it certainly wasn't telling the time now and the bird table was tipped over on its side – I couldn't tell if it was broken or not. I made it my mission, after my bedroom was tidy and organised, that I was going to bring Grandma's garden back to life. It was the right time of year, and I'm sure Mum and Dad would help me buy flowers and shrubs – I would need Dad's help to repair the bird table whilst I was at it as well.

By dinnertime, I had put my books, toys and posters where I wanted them. I was just folding my t-shirts when I overheard Mum and Dad downstairs.

"There you are," I heard Dad say as he walked into the dining room. "Have you been crying? Whatever is the matter? Oh no, no, don't get upset. What has happened?" he sounded anxious now and I wondered if I should go downstairs but then Mum started to talk.

"I'm just remembering a fight Mum and I had here, right here. Oh, it was horrible. The worst. I was ten years old and I was really horrible to her. It was awful and we didn't talk for months afterwards."

"I'm sure she forgave you."

"She said she did. But I'm not sure she ever got over it."

"Do you want to talk about it?"

Dad must've sat down next to her now because his voice was quieter and seemed further away from the door. I, very quietly, crawled to the top of the stairs and listened hard, trying to breathe very lightly as their voices were more muffled. Maybe they were hugging.

"Not really because I can't remember much," Mum replied, "only that my mum was obsessed with magic and fairies and I think she truly believed she was one. When I was just a small girl, I loved her stories, I thrived on them and believed every word she said. That she was the Queen of the fairies and that I was the Princess – I mean what little girl wouldn't love that?" Dad muttered something in agreement. "Anyway – when I was about nine, my friends told me that fairies weren't real and I got upset. That was okay though, because Mum explained that some children don't believe and that was just the way the world was – it just meant that I was special because I believed. Again – fair enough, I could accept that. We would spend hours at a time sat in the garden 'reliving' her stories in make-believe," she paused, "it was wonderful, Ron. It felt so real. But then, sometimes Mum got so lost in her tales that she could get manic and, well, it frightened me – that made her upset and then I started to question if it was real at all. Then, when I was ten, she was telling me one of her stories and I realised that even though they were exotic and rich, they were just that – stories, and I remember telling her. She had one of her crazy minutes and she got very angry and shouted, and I shouted back and said some really nasty things about her being crazy and mental."

I couldn't make out what Dad was saying but he seemed to be comforting Mum. Then, through sobs I heard the next bit, "I realised that everything I thought I knew about my mum was a lie – it couldn't have been true, she had lied to me for years and I wanted to hate her, but she was my mum and I still wanted to feel close to her. She went away on her own for a few weeks, alone. When she came home, I said sorry but she didn't tell me any stories ever again."

"Oh, my love – why have you never told me this before?" my dad questioned.

Mum was still sniffling, "I had forgotten it all – until right now. It all came back to me all of a sudden. I think that perhaps my mum was ill her entire life. I mean, I was devastated that she had lied to me, made me believe in it all… but do you think any person in their right mind would do that to their child?"

There was a hush throughout the house and after about ten minutes, I heard movement in the dining room and so I went back to my room. I was beginning to relate to some of the things I had heard. I knew exactly what Mum had been told because Grandma had told me too. I continued to fold clothes and put shoes away. Mum would need to help me make my bed, though. Pillowcases were one thing but quilt covers were too difficult.

"We're going to have a takeaway, Katie," Dad shouted upstairs, "Come and choose what you want." I trudged downstairs, worried that Mum would still be upset. But she was sorting the wires behind the television in the front room (there were two living rooms in this house, one at the front and one at the back, meaning that whether the sun shone at the front or at the back of the house, it would always warm one of them). I picked up the menu and sat down on the sofa, at least some effort had been made to organise this room.

"I thought we could have a takeaway and watch a film – if I can fathom out these wires," she smiled.

Good, Mum seemed to be okay again. I chose chicken korma and rice for my dinner and then I chose *Alice in Wonderland* for the film. I had a feeling that it was going to be a good first night in our new house after all.

Chapter Four
Helen

I was running through a forest, ducking and diving beneath the low branches and jumping over tree routes. It was as though I was racing with the wind. I laughed, the wind blew and I ran faster to catch up with it. Dragging my Lulu doll behind me, I pressed on. I passed small clearings with pretty flowers where butterflies chased each other and without stopping to watch, I sprinted on. I lifted my hands to my face to stop the twigs scratching my face and eventually, in a small clearing, I stopped and sat down, lungs bursting, hugging my doll to my chest.

I closed my eyes and felt the sunlight warm my skin, I could feel the summer breeze blowing through my hair and I felt relaxed and calm. The sound of wings fluttering danced towards me on the breeze, birdsong filled the air around me and the bees hummed. The small world. It was so beautiful; this was my favourite place in the world. The colours were vibrant and every detail was so clear; I could recall every detail, even with my eyes shut.

As I sat still, I was good at sitting still, with my eyes shut, they came. Pulling apart the leaves and peering through the gaps in hedges, whispering and giggling, "She's back!" and, "Can I play with her?" and, "I wonder if she'll stay this time?" This was the reason I loved this place. This was the reason I came.

I opened my eyes, eager to see their friendly faces.

I sat bolt upright in bed, wide awake and sweating. What on earth was that? What crazy kind of a dream had I just had?

I rubbed my eyes and allowed them to adjust to the dim light. I must've eaten something that disagreed with me. I am no dreamer, and yet that, well, that was something else!

I got out of bed and fumbled in the half-light for my slippers. I pushed my feet into their cosy depth and stood up. Looking at the clock, I noticed that it was 05:45 and I should really try and get some more sleep, I had a busy morning and would be hitting snooze on my alarm in a few hours' time as it was. But still, my mind was far too alert to get back to sleep straight away.

My heart was still racing – as though I really had been running and the backs of my legs were itchy as though the blood had been pumping through my veins. It really was a bizarre sensation, the most realistic dream that I had ever had. I walked downstairs using the glow of the streetlamp outside the glass front door to guide me and I turned on the kitchen light. Flicking the switch on the kettle, I glanced out of the kitchen window and saw the milkman's van turn idly around the corner. I felt oddly uneasy. A cup of tea and a sit down on the sofa would settle me back off to sleep. I made a milky sweet tea and wandered into the living room. I sat on the edge of the sofa and looked out into the garden. There was huge sense of déjà vu, probably because I had sat here many times over the last 39 years.

There was a photograph of my mum on the wall adjacent to the patio doors and I relaxed into the settee – looking at her face and smiling. She was a wonderful woman. I knew that we had had our ups and downs but apart from that one fallout and the few years of unrest that had followed, we had gotten on marvellously – more like best friends than mother-daughter. I finished my cup of tea still looking at her. I really missed her. I took my cup into the kitchen and rinsed it in the sink and took myself back to bed, pausing to look at Katie through the gap in her door. I snuggled into the warmth of my bed and closed my eyes, drifting back to sleep with ease.

Chapter Five
Katie

I rolled over in my bed, the warm morning sunlight streaming through the bedroom window. The house was quiet and still. It took my eyes a few minutes to come into focus but I could see the dust fairies dancing in the straight lines of light. Fairies. I smiled – I had dreamt of the most wonderful things in the night. I focussed for a moment, allowing the dream to surface and come clear in my mind.

A small girl, no bigger than six or seven was running through the lush, long, green grass of a forest filled with enchanted beings. The blue bells and daffodils nodded at her as she bounded past, her ragdoll being dragged along behind her. She was smiling and laughing, running on through the bush, eager to get to her destination. She lifted her arms and used them to push twigs out of her face. And then, when she reached its small clearing, she sat down abruptly, pulled her doll to her chest and closed her eyes. She looked happy, at peace and – I mused – a little familiar. I looked at the doll and instantly recognised it – there was one like that in our attic – how strange! The little girl sat patiently, so patiently, her eyes scrunched closed as if waiting for the surprise that she knew would appear at any minute. I heard a whisper close behind me, "She's back," turning around to look, I heard, "Can I play with her?"

There was a giggle and a sigh, I saw a little girl, twinkling eyes and rosy cheeks; she was pretty. From the smile on her face and the look in her eye, I just knew she would know so

many fun games and that I could have so much fun with her –
she seemed to be very much like me.

"I wonder if she'll stay this time," I heard another voice
remark slightly louder.

I awoke at this point and a bizarre sense of familiarity
came over me – although I had never had this dream before, I
still felt like there was something about this dream that wasn't
new to me. I thought about the doll, the same as the one in the
attic. I had helped Dad to put the boxes in the loft and had
seen the doll with my own eyes. It had been Mum's when she
was a little girl and I had seen photographs in Grandma's
photo album. Perhaps that was the reason I had dreamt about
it. The human brain has a fantastic way of filing memories
away.

I sat up, stretched and manoeuvred my legs over the side
of the bed. Putting on my slippers and dressing gown, I
hesitated at the door – there was no noise or movement from
inside Mum and Dad's room so I assumed that they were still
asleep; they had probably continued to unpack boxes well into
the night so I tiptoed downstairs and into the living room. The
clock told me that it was still quite early; 7:30 but already the
garden looked alive in the morning light. I pulled some of the
cushions from the sofa onto the floor and wrapped myself up,
snug in my old dressing gown and I plonked myself at the
patio doors and lay down. I looked straight up the garden
towards the hedgerows and bushes at the far end. Questions
floated in and out of my mind as I lay in the morning warmth
of summer.

I thought back to my dream, I knew that little girl, I knew
I did. I just couldn't place her. The warmth of the sunlight and
the fact that I had woken up so early after a much later than
usual night meant that my eyes grew tired. I closed them,
smiling and drifted into a peaceful doze.

"Katie! What on earth are you sleeping down here for?"

Mum had walked into the living room to a pile of cushions
and me, her little girl, snoozing in the sunlight; looking like
an angel (she always described me as an angel). She loved my

rosy cheeks and pink lips on my pale white skin and blonde hair sprawling in ringlets.

Yawning and stretching, I sat up, still warm and suddenly very thirsty, "Morning," I croaked and smiled, eyes tempted to close again. "Can I have a drink please, Mum?"

She offered me her glass of orange juice as she sat on the sofa. Oh it was good! I gulped it down in three big mouthfuls. Sweet, fresh orange juice. Mum always had to buy the 'no bits' juice just for me because I didn't like the bits in the one that they preferred. Once my thirst was quenched, I stood up and passed Mum the cushions one by one and then planted myself next to her on the sofa.

Thinking about how things would change now that we were living here, I asked Mum one of the questions that was pressing on my mind, "What time will I have to get up for school living here?" I knew that we were a little closer to Dad's work, that was one of the benefits of living here but I wasn't sure about school. "Can I walk there or do I need to get the bus?"

Mum smiled at me. She loved that I was conscientious about school and that I was academically minded, already planning for school after the holidays, even though they had barely begun.

"I will take you on my way to work for the first few weeks," Mum said, "then you can decide if you want to walk some days." She put her arm around me and pulled me close. "I think we're going to be happy here, Katie."

"Yep, me too," I agreed. "We just need to do something about the garden!"

We both laughed.

That morning, we pulled on our wellies (after locating the box that they were packed in) and started the garden. Pulling up weeds was hard work. I knew that if the plants I pulled came out easily, they were probably not weeds and the ones that I struggled with probably were – which was ironic. We decided between us, that we both should have listened more to Grandma – neither of us could recall the names of the bushes and flowers. Before lunch, we took it in turns to push the petrol lawnmower back and forwards. It was a little heavy for my small arms and short legs so Mum had to do most of it and I raked up the cuttings and put them in the wheelie bin as she did.

Dad continued to empty boxes in the house. Glad that we were out of the way, he could do his organising in peace. He waved at us from the window now and then and by the time he called us in for lunch – chip shop chips and curry (because the kitchen still wasn't properly unpacked). As we went indoors, I turned to look at our work so far and yes, mowing the lawn and de-weeding the boarders had already started to make a difference. As I stepped through the patio doors, I glanced at the rhododendrons at the bottom of the garden and remembered my grandma standing there in her apron a few years ago. I smiled.

Chapter Six
Katie

It was the end of the summer holidays; tomorrow I would be going back to school – and into year six. I was both nervous and excited. I wondered if my new teacher would be as kind as Mrs Potts last year.

I was sat in the living room and the television was on but I wasn't watching. Instead, I was musing over what a wonderful summer we had just had; the house now looked and felt like home and the garden had been made to look like Grandma's garden again, the flowers were bright and colourful and the weather had been lovely enough for us to have had a couple of barbecues and we even sunbathed on a couple of days. It had been a glorious summer and I felt ready for the routine and regularity that school would bring.

Later that evening, whilst gazing at our handiwork, I realised that I was glad that I had asked Dad to move the bird table after he had fixed it. Previously, it had been at the bottom of the garden but now it stood in pride of place in front of the patio doors so that I could watch the birds land and eat their fill. I would be easily able to re-stash it with all the different treats I was planning to make – I had been online and had made a list of all the ingredients I would need to make the most delicious snacks the birds would ever eat their fill of.

Mum had cooked chicken and sweetcorn pasta bake for dinner and my belly was full. I was watching the little lights (maybe fireflies, I wasn't sure) at the far end of the garden, they flitted to and fro between the bushes. I wasn't sure what was creating the lights, maybe reflections from the streetlights, but it was very pretty.

"Go and make your sandwiches," Dad instructed. It was my job now that I was going into the final year of primary school – to promote independence and to encourage me to take control of the things that were mine.

"There is plenty of choice in the fridge," Mum added.

I dragged myself away from the dancing fairy-lights and did as I was told. I took the bread out of the bread bin and the butter out of the fridge. I buttered two slices of bread and smeared on the sandwich filler from the jar; wrapped them in foil and put them in my lunchbox, I also threw in a bag of plain crisps and a chocolate muffin. Mum would probably not approve of my less-than-healthy lunch, but once I zipped it up, no one would be checking anyway. With this menial task done, I wandered back into the living room and sat down once again to stare at the lights at the bottom of the garden.

They were gone. I felt a pang of disappointment in my stomach and sighed.

"What's up, Katie?" Mum asked.

"The little lights have gone," I grumbled, "They were there before I went into the kitchen and now they're gone."

Mum looked confused, "What lights?"

"The fireflies at the end of the garden."

"Fireflies?" Dad seemed interested, "Are they the same as glowworms?" he mused.

Mum was quick to reply, "I doubt they are, sweetheart. They don't tend to come out this late in the year."

Both Dad and I were shocked at Mum's knowledge on this matter and shared a look. "Don't be so surprised, you two!" she chuckled. "My mum was Queen of the fairies, remember!" She threw her head back and laughed, Dad joined in and I watched on at them, unsure as to whether it was appropriate for them to be laughing at my dead grandmother, especially in front of me.

Chapter Seven
Helen

I think that I must have offended Katie with my comment about Mum. Her face dropped in the split second it took me to start laughing. Then Ron had joined in and I thought that she might cry.

"I'm off to bed, night," she said quietly and off she went.

I felt bad for a moment. My little girl clearly loved her grandmother – well, the memory of her – and my comment had hurt her. I reprimanded myself and promised not to talk about or laugh at my mother's madness, which is what I had decided had been wrong with her for the many years leading up to her diagnosis. I turned to Ron, smiled and kissed his shoulder.

"I love you."

"I love you, too," he replied, and we sat in the lamplight, together, holding hands as the remainder of the daylight faded and the garden grew blacker.

Ron turned off the TV a short while later and I read my book as he played word games on his kindle; my feet kicked over his legs as we both sat on the sofa. Life was pretty perfect right now. We were living in my childhood home, there was no mortgage left on it and we were renting out our house across town. We were in a better financial situation than we could ever have wished for. I smiled a contented smile. Out of the corner of my eye, a small light flickered; I turned my head to try and focus on what it was, but it was gone. Strange. If Katie had seen fireflies – or glow bugs as I had called them as a child, then they were out of season and out of sync with the weather. Again, I chuckled at my knowledge of such trivial things – I was well and truly my mother's daughter.

That night in bed, I dreamt again.

Different this time to last.

I was stood with my mother in the garden. Her long blond hair fell in ringlets about her smiling, radiant face. She wore a very simple yet elegant white dress that draped off her shoulder and sat in pleats around her bare feet. I was just thinking to myself how much Katie looked like her, the same hair and eyes, and she said aloud, "I think that all the time."

I was shocked. "How did you know what I was thinking?"

"We faeries have many gifts, Helen!" She loved to use my name when she spoke to me, I loved it too. "You know," she paused, "we've had this same conversation many times now."

'Have we?' I thought.

She smiled. "Yet still, you have not met me here once in person – only ever in your dreams. You have not made a single effort to find me. Even when you were working in the garden with Katie... It looks lovely by the way. I am so pleased that Katie liked the old sundial," she paused, "and that she wanted Ronald to fix the bird table, the birds are happy to feed here again."

I was roused from my dream at this point as Katie got up for the toilet. That was strange. My dreams were getting so lifelike – I must try and get to bed earlier, I was clearly very tired.

Katie

My heart was pounding, I was sweating and my cheeks were flushed. I stood looking in the mirror and the more I looked at myself, the more I saw my grandma, the Grandma who I had *just* seen standing *with* my mum, in the garden. Our garden, the way we had just left it today; bird table in front of the patio doors, no longer hidden at the bottom of the garden, now in full plain sight. I opened the bathroom window and leant out to see if she was still stood there – my dream had been so real – but the night was dark and even the stars were hiding behind clouds. I closed the window and climbed down from the side of the bath. Splashing my face with cool water, I took one last look in the mirror and left the bathroom, pulling the cord and switching off the light.

At the bottom of the garden, a pair of eyes smiled and watched the bathroom light go off. It was time.

Chapter Eight
Katie

The first week of school came and went without incident. On Monday morning, I looked in the mirror and noticed that my face had a healthy glow to it – all the sunshine and time outdoors had given me a tan. Dad even commented that he thought I might have grown over the summer and then added that it was probably because I had been stood in the flowerbeds all summer as though I had sprouted roots or something – my dad thinks that he is hilarious.

My hair had grown an inch or two and Mum had scraped it back into a bobble to keep it out of my way. She dropped me off at school every morning and I walked home each afternoon. Being ever studious, I worked hard, did my homework and, on the whole, enjoyed the challenges that year six brought. I still drove the teachers mad with my immature handwriting. I slept well at nights. The work at school, the homework and the reading were wearing me out and making my brain tired. Yet, I felt energetic each morning and ready for the day. I didn't dream much, there wasn't time.

On Friday after school, I decided that I wanted to spend time in the garden over the weekend, I was already missing it. I wanted to draw and paint the flowers, to lie in the sunshine and listen to the birds in their nests and the crickets in the tall grass. I wanted to use the time to think about my grandma and how much she had loved her garden. I also wanted to think over my dream, very real dream – with my grandma and my mum.

Saturday awoke gloriously, with the sun bright from dawn until dusk. I rose early, had breakfast at the kitchen table and headed outside with my colouring books and sketchpad. I set up my 'area' close to the sundial – I loved to watch the shadow moving. It was also my grandma's favourite garden ornament, so, considering that I was going to be thinking a lot about her today – decided to sit close by. I closed my eyes for a moment and enjoyed the warmth of the rays beating down on my face. I saw flickering dots dancing on the backs of my eyelids, I could hear the breeze rustling through the leaves and knew that on opening my eyes, they would look as though they were dancing and frolicking in their boughs. There was a feeling of magic in that moment. I loved it. I sat for a while, enjoying the sounds and smells of our garden, Grandma's garden, thinking of all the stories Grandma had told me.

After lunch of quiche and new potatoes, I went back into the garden. The sun was now blocked by the roof of next-door's house and I was sat in shade, so I moved my chair around the flowerbeds to find a better spot. I spent another hour sketching the hydrangeas on the closest bush. They were intricate little flowers bunched together to look like one big flower. Ours were pink and lilac. According to the sundial, it took me about 45 minutes to draw it and then, for fifteen minutes I set up my watercolours and filled an old jam jar with water from the hosepipe.

I concentrated very hard on the different shades of blues and lilac, the green of the leaves and the stalks. I saw a butterfly hover over my paper, enticed by the pretty colours no doubt but then realising that they were not real flowers nor did they contain sweet nectar.

As the sun bore down on me, my eyelids became heavy and I felt sleepy. I lay my brush aside as I closed my eyes.

I could still see the butterfly, it danced merrily above my paper and then it landed in the wet paint. As it wandered about the paper, its tiny feet left a trail on the page. It wasn't afraid at all. It opened and closed its colourful wings a couple of times and looked over at me as if beckoning me to follow. On the next gust of warm, summer air, the butterfly took off; it circled in front of me and then dived towards the hydrangeas, I followed with my eyes. As it sat on a flower, the breeze moved the bush ever so slightly, and I thought I saw a small door, only about ten centimetres tall – but perfectly formed with a handle and a window. A regular-looking, old-fashioned front door. It was cut into the thickest part of the hydrangea stalk. I blinked, rubbed my eyes and looked again, but it was gone.

The cool breeze woke me. The sun had started to sink behind the fence at the end of the garden and its warmth had gone. Although I still felt warm in my half-sleeping state as I sat up. I looked at my painting, I was improving, there was much more detail in this one, I was smiling at it when, on the top of one petal, I noticed tiny, dark-blue flecks that were dotted all over the top right-hand section, my mind peeled back to my dream – the butterfly? No! I shouldn't be so silly – I was about to get cross at myself when I had the strange sensation that I was being watched. I glanced at the house. No one was there, not at any of the back windows. I could hear Dad in the living room laughing at something he was watching on TV and Mum was probably cooking dinner. I looked at the hydrangea, my eyes moving lower until, with the last light of sunshine, I saw the wings of the very same butterfly sitting on the lowest flower and I could swear it was looking right at me.

Leaning forward to look closer, I knocked over the jam jar with my paintbrushes in them and as they fell to the floor, the butterfly flew into the bush for shelter. I knelt down to retrieve my brushes and a cold shiver travelled down my spine. I could hear my grandmother's voice inside my head as clear as if she was standing behind me,

"Underneath the lowest bows and between the twigs and rocks, there exists – only to those who believe – a small door to a world beyond your imagination. Always believe, Katie, and it will be."

Pretending to reach under the bush for my brushes, I moved the lowest stalks to one side and gasped.

There was the door.

Chapter Nine
Helen

I flinched as Katie knocked over her brushes, she would be cross at that. She didn't like disorder or feeling clumsy. I watched as she crouched down at the back of the garden to pick them up. Dinner was ready – chicken and mushroom risotto. I opened the patio doors and leant out.

"Dinner is ready, Katie, do you need a hand?"

"I'm okay," she replied – not in her usual chipper voice.

I walked down the path and as she turned around, I could see straight away that my baby girl was not well. She was pale and her skin shone slightly in the last of the sunlight. I felt her head. It was dry and hot; she definitely had a temperature.

"When was the last time you had a drink, Katie?"

Her head turned to me and her eyes drifted lazily back again, she opened her mouth and vomited on my feet. My arm caught her before she keeled over.

"Ron!" I shouted in alarm. "Ron, help me please." I was supporting Katie's weight in one arm whilst holding her art things in the other and trying to move away from the pile of vomit at the same time.

"Wha…" He saw her and ran. "Come here, let me take her." Katie was in his arms now, looking floppy and so much younger than she was.

"Heat stroke?" I half stated, half-questioned as I looked at Ron, feeling utterly devastated that I had not brought Katie in from the garden earlier.

"Let's get her into the house, Helen," he calmly yet firmly spoke.

I kicked off my shoes, put Katie's art things just inside the door and climbed through, not caring about the vomit all over me.

Katie didn't get poorly often and it was a shock to both Ron and myself at seeing her so ill. He lay her on the sofa, and she opened her eyes and they fluttered shut again.

"Mum!" she cried, "I'm going to be sick again."

I ran to get a bowl from the kitchen, arriving back just in time. Then, I went to the bathroom to get a cool flannel and a towel.

Katie threw up three more times, she wouldn't drink, afraid of being sick again, so she lay on the sofa for the evening with a cold flannel on her forehead and the breeze from the garden cooling her down. Ron, who was such a good dad, sat on the floor near her head and I sat on the sofa with her feet on my lap. And that is where we sat as we watched Saturday night television and where Katie slept and, eventually, where Ron and I ate warmed-up chicken and mushroom risotto.

Katie slept well that night, I checked on her every half hour. Her temperature came down so I calmed and became less paranoid and we put her to bed at ten o'clock.

Chapter Ten
Katie

I was standing at the door. I knocked. Nothing. I knocked again. Still nothing. Would it be rude to walk in without an invitation? I knocked one last time, just in case. Nothing. Taking a deep breath, I reached out my hand and placed my palm flat onto the warm wood. Pushing gently, the door opened, a warm breeze hit and blew my hair and dress backwards. I stepped back in alarm and saw something blue in the corner of my eye. I turned my head and saw the butterfly. It floated on down to me and beckoned me with its large gentle eyes to follow. He (I assumed it was a he) folded up his wings and stepped through the door. I was amazed at his size. I mean, with his wings standing proud on his back, he was as tall as me. Either I had shrunk considerably or he had grown. I halted in my step and looked at the door, the tiny door, too small for a child, I had seen it earlier and had just walked through it...

"When was the last time you had a drink, Katie?" A wave of heat passed over me as though I was going to be sick, I sat down. I heard a commotion behind me.

"Ron!" I heard my mum's voice as clear as day and a moment later, I was standing again. I walked a little further. I heard voices, whispering, and children? The butterfly had taken flight again and was floating elegantly in the air above my head. I followed its shadow on the floor. This place was beautiful. I could hear people but whenever I looked in the direction of the voices, they stopped. I walked on, unperturbed. I felt at home. Unafraid with a sense of déjà vu. I had been here before – I was sure of it.

As I walked, the grass and the flowers seemed to watch me. The bluebells and snowdrops nodded their delicate heads at me and there was an abundance of colour. It really was a beautiful place. I followed the shadow of the blue butterfly. A few moments longer and the flowers and grass became scarcer and there was a flat stone area – almost like a patio or a stage or platform. It was circular in shape and could easily have been a meeting place. The butterfly had landed a short way in front of me and appeared to be having a rest. I found a lump of wood near to the centre of the barren patch of land and sat down upon it.

Before I had even placed my full weight onto my makeshift resting place, there was a gasp of pain or surprise from somewhere behind me and I stood up quickly, checking over my shoulder. Something moved and I walked away to the other side. I waited and waited. I sat down on the floor. I rested my forehead in my palms, propped my elbows on my knees, closed my eyes and thought hard. 'Why was I here? What was I supposed to do?' I knew I was dreaming, I was lucid enough for that but at the same time, I felt connected to this place and that I was here for a reason. So I waited.

I closed my eyes and tried hard to listen to the voices that floated on the breeze towards me. "She looks just like her."

"I wonder if she knows."

"I can't wait to see her – I'm so excited!"

I kept my eyes closed, aware that the voices were getting closer and I couldn't be certain but I was beginning to get the feeling that I was no longer alone; I was right. Within a few moments, I was aware of many feet walking on the stones, groups of people and creatures, huddling, waiting for the same thing as me? I wasn't sure. I was tempted to open my eyes but I was both too excited and too afraid to see what I could hear and feel around me.

I didn't have to wait long.

There was a sudden hush. A stillness that could not be explained in any other word than reverence. And then she spoke – directly to me, my grandma.

"You can open your eyes, Katie."

It was morning again when I woke up, I had a dry mouth and my throat hurt. Mum had put a bucket at the side of the bed, which I hadn't needed. As soon as my temperature had come down, I had been fine. I sat up and looked around the room. I spotted my sketchpad at the bottom of the bed and reached for it. I opened it to the painting from yesterday. I ran my fingers over the speckles of paint in the corner and my mind ran through the events of the following afternoon. And to the dream – if that is what it was. I could no longer distinguish between reality and dreams. I sank from the bed to the floor, hugging my knees and resting my head on them. There was so much to process, to come to terms with. The world that I thought I knew was only the smallest part of a bigger and much more intricate painting.

"I made the choice to leave my human form behind to come here. To come home because," my grandmother had explained to me once formal introductions and explanations had been made, "my people needed me to ensure their survival."

I had been invited to walk with the woman who I had adored in her human form and now whom I adored, even more, for her decision, her passion, her love and for sharing it with me. It turned out that my bloodline, my lineage, for over a hundred centuries before my birth had been linked with another world, another creation and a life that only a few are privileged to know about. I wasn't even shocked or scared about it. It was almost as though somewhere deep inside I had known it all along.

The Keepers of the Earth; the painters of flowers; the planters of seeds; the friends of birds and bees and butterflies (they go by many names); live a quiet life at the very heart of nature. They are responsible for the continuation of life. They make it their responsibility to care for the roots that feed the trees that breathe out the oxygen required for the survival of the planet. They nurture and care for all plants, painting the petals of each flower as it blossoms and blooms, making each one beautiful and desirable to the insects that visit and pollinate. They were the Keepers of the Earth – fairies to you and, formerly, to me – and my grandmother was Queen of them all.

Way back, before even my grandmother's grandmother was born, there was a small group of like-minded people. People who cared deeply about the Earth and wanted to keep it safe from harm. They were laughed at for their efforts and so, for their own peace, they lived in the forests, they built tree houses and established communities away from the cities that were polluting the Earth; they continued the work that they loved; they became one with the planet. Over the years, as technology became more used and as the world began to destroy itself, these caring people were forgotten about. As nature was replaced with industry, green with grey, they grew smaller in size yet larger in number; they made their world and their impact bigger. They vanished from sight only because people did not care to look for them and yet, they still cared for a world that could not care for itself. They lived for longer and the world returned the favour and offered them sanctity and solitude within itself. The work of a faerie is still, to this day, to love and to nurture and to care for the land. Those who open their eyes and believe are the small few who are privileged to see the true beauty of it all and to not be perturbed by the reality of it all.

I was one of those few; it was exciting and yet I was nervous. Mum had thought my grandmother had been mad, that she had lied to her and that small misunderstanding had, over the years, very nearly destroyed their relationship. I wasn't sure what I was supposed to do with the information now that I had it, it wasn't the sort of thing that you could forget but neither was it something that could be easily talked about. It was strange that even though I knew that I had seen all of this in a dream, there was no doubt in my mind that it was real.

Now that I knew the basics, I needed to know more. I hadn't asked any questions at the time, but now, back in my world, my head was filled with so many. Did Grandpa know? Why did Mum not believe when I knew from dreams that she had been there as a child? Why had I been able to see and get through the door? Would I have to make a similar decision to leave this life?

Feeling confused and, now that I came to think of it – hungry, I stuffed my feet into my slippers and wrapped my dressing gown around me. Mum and Dad were still upstairs, I could hear them talking about some of Mum's friends from work. I walked quietly down the stairs and into the living room. I lay on the sofa and looked out through the patio windows. There were birds feeding at the bird table and I could see butterflies fluttering around the bushes at the bottom of the garden. I wondered if she was watching me now. She told me that she had visited me every night since we had moved in and that she was working on Mum too. She needed Mum to remember something although she wouldn't explain to me what it was or why it was so important.

Chapter Eleven
Katie

There was an uncomfortable air in the house, I wasn't sure if anyone else felt it or if it was just me being paranoid. Perhaps they just put my quietness down to being poorly the previous evening because I couldn't make conversation and I didn't want to let slip about meeting my grandma; I knew that they would worry and think that my being ill was causing me to see things, or they may think that I had inherited some family madness. Either way, I found it easier to not speak and let them think that I was recovering. It gave me time to think things through and that worked well for me. What I needed, however, was someone to talk to.

I was limited in this department; I wasn't a social butterfly. I found it difficult to talk to people when it meant opening up to them as I was an innately private person. I had friends, those that I talked to at school and I was happy to talk about school and clubs and homework; I shied away from talking about boys – thankfully, those conversations were limited to celebrities and boy bands and I could busy myself doing other stuff and they would put this down to my lack of interest in social media. I didn't hang out with school friends outside of school either – I liked to come home and spend time with my family and most of all, to read books. This was even more the case now that we had moved and I lived considerably further away from those I knew well.

Apart from my mum and dad, there wasn't anyone that I could speak to. I wondered if that made me 'socially awkward' and had a little chuckle to myself. If I had been socially awkward before, I would be even more so now, I smiled to myself.

"It's nice to see you smiling, Katie," Mum remarked as she brought me a plate of toast and jam. "What do you want to do today?"

"Stay in my pyjamas and watch a movie." It was my favourite thing to do when I felt grumpy, sad or tired or when I just didn't want to talk.

"Then that is fine by me. You gave us a fright last night, so eat some toast and if you can keep it down, I will put whatever film you want on." She headed for the kitchen, "Tea?"

"Juice please," I replied.

"Dad is going to play golf later on today, so if you think that you will be okay on your own for an hour, I might pop over to see Grandad – I haven't seen him this week."

GRANDAD! Of course. I could talk to Grandad.

I would need to engineer a plan to get there without Mum or Dad, but it was perfect. He wouldn't laugh at me – even if he didn't believe me. I knew this because he hadn't ever laughed at Grandma. So that was the plan. I would find an excuse to visit grandpa on my own. Feeling more settled in my decision, I relaxed and ate my toast, which of course, I managed to keep down.

It was just over a week later that both Mum and Dad were working late and I was instructed to make my own way home from school. So, instead of walking straight home from the bus stop, I walked to the care home where my grandpa now lived. Tree-Tops was the best care home in the area and, where most care homes were known for being less than caring, Grandpa assured us that he was 'very well looked after, thank you very much' and that we should be more worried about the way he treated the staff and not the way the staff treated him. He would chuckle as he said it and we never knew quite what he meant but he seemed cheerful and happy whenever we came to see him. He smiled and waved as I walked through the foyer.

"What a lovely surprise, Katie!" he beamed at me. "Come closer and let me see how you look." I gave him a squeeze and posed and turned a circle in front of him, he sat me on his knee and whispered, "Just like my Elsie." He kissed my cheek and gestured for me to pull up a chair.

As I sat, he looked at me, "I know that look, Katie, something bothering you?"

I didn't know where to start. So I spoke honestly and briefly, "I've been having dreams about Grandma, I think they're real, they feel real but I'm not sure if they are or not." To my surprise, he did not look shocked or troubled. Before he spoke, he took off his glasses, lay them on the table next to him and rubbed his eyes.

"She's been visiting you too, then?"

"What? You too, Grandpa?"

"She told me she would," his voice was lowered, almost to a whisper and I had to lean forward in my chair to hear him properly, "I'm just glad you took it better than your mother did," he shook his head.

Okay, not quite what I was expecting. I was more confused than ever. Not only did Grandpa not question me, not think I was having elaborate daydreams, but he knew it was happening and had been expecting me to come to him. I was shocked and couldn't speak. Grandpa put his hand over to his shirt pocket and pulled out a small red cube with a white button on it. He pressed it once and put it back into his pocket. Within moments a short, red-haired lady was heading over to him.

She smiled and crouched down to speak to him, "Is everything okay, Ted?"

"Yes, thank you," he replied, "My granddaughter and I would like to have a pot of tea in my room, please." He smiled at her and she nodded.

"Do you want a chair to get there?"

"That would be a grand idea," he smirked back.

Five minutes later, I was pushing my grandpa down the corridor to his room. It was a fairly blandly decorated room; white walls, two paintings, a small bed in the corner, a couple of day chairs and a small table by the window that over looked the garden. I was glad to see that some of Grandpa's books had made it here with him and were stacked haphazardly on the small bookcase. He transferred himself to one of the chairs and pulled a blanket over his knees. There was a knock at the door and the same red-haired woman opened the door; a tray in her hands with a pot of tea, two teacups and a plate of biscuits,

"All yours, Ted," she smiled. She placed the tray on the table and left again. "Shout if you need anything. Anything at all." She winked at him and closed the door.

Chapter Twelve
Katie

In silence, Grandpa poured two cups of tea and then sat back in his chair, "So…" he paused, I could feel his eyes penetrating mine, "I had a feeling this day would come. And to be fair, I'm glad it has come whilst I am still in control of my mind enough to help. At least you will know that what I tell you is real."

I nodded, waiting for him to continue.

"Your grandma was a very special lady. She knew her lineage before I met her and she was always very honest with me," he chuckled, "I was either too in love to fully understand when she told me or I was the perfect match," he paused, "I like to think the latter."

"You knew all along?"

"Oh yes, Katie, and I was privileged to go to Hafan too. It made it easier to let her go when the time came. I knew that I wasn't really losing her and that she would still come and see me when she could." He drank his tea and picked up a biscuit. Playing with it and dropping crumbs into his lap, he looked at me, "But that is not what we need to discuss now. I have a lot to explain and I am assuming your mother doesn't know that you are here?"

I hid my face and blushed.

"Pass me that leather-bound diary from the bottom shelf please, Katie."

It was the book that I remembered from my childhood visits to their home. The books that I had always been drawn to but that had always been out of reach. I did as I was asked and sat back down, watching Grandpa unwind the leather cord that held the book closed with his bony white hands. He thumbed through the pages until he found what he was looking for.

He cleared his throat, "March 3rd, 1978."

"Mum's birthday," I whispered.

He nodded without looking up. "What a wonderful day and a celebration of life. Baby Helen Louise Scott was born at 17:01. My beautiful faerie princess…" Still without looking up, he skimmed a few pages forward. "Formal introductions were made and Helen was loved by all. Mummy is very excited that we have a girl. It will ensure our lineage once more." He turned a few pages more, "March 3rd, 1981. For Helen's third birthday, even Edward – that's me –" he looked at me and winked, "was privileged to join us in the Hafan. What a wonderful family experience."

"You went there a lot?" I questioned.

"Only a few times. I would love to go back," he lowered his head, "but I am too old now and I fear that my tired body would not survive the transition. But oh how I loved it when your grandma would take me to meet her family. It truly is the place of dreams." He handed me the book. "Have a little read," he suggested.

June 10th, 1985

Helen didn't want to come home today, she cried as we left. She spent most of the day polishing bluebells and riding butterflies. I am sure that she will transition well when the time comes. She belongs to our world – that much is clear. Elsie x.

There were more entries, every couple of months had seen my grandma document the coming and goings of her daughter in the faerie world – or Hafan – literally translating from our ancestral tongue to a place of safety and refuge for those who cared deeply about the natural world. Each entry was signed by my grandma with a kiss.

There were flowers and blades of grass pressed between the pages, sometimes smudging the words and she had drawn the most beautiful images of flowers and fairies, creatures and landscapes; each page was decorated and coloured with so much detail. My artistic talent must run in the family. And it was clear that my grandma must have spent a lot of time close to nature allowing her to see this much detail. I loved it. It was like a scrapbook of my grandma's secret and mother's childhood – a memoir if you would.

Then I saw the photographs, such beautiful images, taken of the bottom of the garden. I looked closer, I knew that bush, I lowered my head to the image and I could see the door carved into the bark and as I squinted, Grandpa passed me a magnifying glass. I was confused for one second and then grasped it from him and looked even closer at the image. There, sat just outside the door, in rows like a school photo were all my grandma's family, sitting next to her mother, a very beautiful faerie (my great-grandmother, Esme), she held a small child on her lap – my mum. All fairies, every single one. Such a beautiful picture of a garden and to the more discerning eye – a family portrait.

"I took that picture when your mum was just five years old. It's is the only copy I have."

"Keep it safe, Grandpa," I whispered back.

I kept flicking through, not reading, but eyes wandering in amazement and stopped when one entry caught my eye. It was splattered with water and some of the inky words were smudged. It didn't have the same happy tone about it.

<u>March 3rd, 1988</u>

Words cannot express fully the heartbreak that I feel. It is entirely my fault, I am sure. My mother will be most upset. Who knows what she will do now to rectify the situation; I have endangered us all. To my utter dismay, Helen cannot recall any of the visits to Hafan and believes the memories are simply fairy-tale that I have told. She cannot comprehend a world other than this dull one and I have no idea what to do. The winter away has seen her grow up too fast and her ability to believe in magic is gone...

It continued but I didn't read on.

Hurriedly, forehead creased and brows dipped, I flicked back to find out what had happened as my grandma was clearly very distraught about it. I only had to read a couple of entries to find out why. There were no entries from September to February in the diary. Everything was March to July and sometimes August. August 1987 answered it for me.

August 9th, 1987

How have I raised such a beautiful kind and caring child? It really is a privilege to call her mine. She has such a love of creatures and was seen talking to an old earthworm today and then sat in a web using it as a hammock. I have never seen anyone so comfortable around the spiders before. She helped the other faerie babies clean the grass shoots and sang them to sleep when they got tired, she helped our elders filter the soil and water the deep roots of the tree. Lying on a leaf, she watched as we flew to and fro collecting essentials for the colder months, she laughed and smiled and sang. Such a helpful and delightful child; she seems to like it here. She will miss this place over the winter, I'm sure, but she has not yet grown accustomed to our lifestyle and she will feel the bitter pinch of winter. I will return with her in the spring when she can paint the flowers and add colour to the world.

Saying goodbye to my mother was hard. She has enjoyed seeing so much of me and Helen. I have assured her that one more year and Helen will be a permanent resident at the Hafan. Next in line to the throne and the promise that our world can continue once Mummy can no longer lead.

It was the next bit that I read where realisation struck.

'How can such a small being hold so much responsibility on her shoulders and be unaware? My child will be Queen of the Hafan one day and will ensure the survival of our kind…' What a wonderful thought that is.

Elsie x

"Is that why Grandma had to go back? Because Mum didn't?" I asked in a whisper.

"Yes, darling. Your grandma was very angry with herself for a long while and I think your mum always felt that it was her fault. They didn't get on very well for a long while after that," he explained.

"Poor Mum," I paused. "Poor Grandma," I added.

"Things got better once you arrived though. And it warmed my heart when your mum let your Grandma help look after you."

"Do you miss her, Grandpa?"

"Sometimes. But," he paused and closed his eyes for a moment, "I get a visit from a beautiful blue butterfly every now and then. My eyes may not be spectacular but I know she is riding it and watching me."

"Do you…" I paused and cleared my throat, "Do you wish that you had gone too?"

"I couldn't if I wanted to, Katie dear, I was only permitted access out of love. It is not in my genetic makeup to live their life. And besides, I had to be here to tell you all of this and," he paused, "deliver this to you. Didn't I?" He handed me the diary, now all neatly tied back up.

I smiled, then beamed, "This is for me?"

"Yes, keep it safe."

I sat for another ten minutes or so, just thinking before realising the time. I kissed Grandpa on his head and darted towards that door, turning when I got there, as there was a niggling thought in the back of my mind, "Grandpa, shouldn't I be feeling strange?"

"What do you mean, Katie?"

"I mean, Grandma died and now she's not – I am the granddaughter of a faerie… Shouldn't that feel odd?"

"For some people, perhaps, but you know more than them. You believe and that makes your mind more able to comprehend that sort of magic."

I beamed. I liked that thought. Closing the door behind me, I ran home as quickly as I could.

It wasn't until I was sat on my bed at home that I processed and made sense of everything that Grandpa had said. I read some more of the diary. It was quite an amazing situation to get my head around. As for what I thought I had worked out about the state of my future; high school, college, university… That was all about to change and, according to Grandpa's insinuations, I wasn't sure I wanted to believe the conclusion I came to. I had to tell Mum.

I waited until after dinner that evening, until Dad had gone to the pub and Mum was folding the laundry. I spoke calmly and precisely, trying to carefully think about every word. I had the diary with me in case I needed it. I had never been very good with words and I doubted that this would be any different. She wasn't going to believe what I had to say.

Chapter Thirteen
Katie

"I know about Grandma, Mum." I went straight in there.

"What about Grandma?" she asked, without even flinching.

"I know the truth. Grandpa told me."

She lifted her eyes, "When did you see Grandpa? And what truth? Katie, you'll have to explain what you are talking about. I have had a long day at work and my brain isn't as sharp as usual."

"I know about the Hafan."

"The what?"

"Where Grandma lives now."

Eyes wide, Mum sat on the bed reaching out and checking my forehead to see if I was ill again. "Katie, you have lost me completely now." She looked tired and I knew that I wasn't being very tactful.

"Mum, I know that as a child, you were meant to go and live at the Hafan, to take over from your grandmother as leader of the Keepers of the Earth."

"Keepers of the – what?" Mum looked really confused. I mean, she didn't know what I was talking about.

"Mum, I know that you went there. I read Grandma's diary, I have Grandma's diary. What are you hiding from me and why?"

She put her head in her hands. She had no words. She literally didn't have the slightest clue what I was talking about.

"Read it, Mum," I placed the book on the bed next to her, "and then tell me that Grandma was lying all along."

Feeling confused and a little hurt – how could anyone forget something so magical? I went to my room and closed the door. Something wasn't right. Mum should remember things that happened to her at my age. How could you forget something not just magical, but so perfect, so real and so beautiful? It was the stuff dreams were made of. Every girl would kill for the chance to be a princess, heir to a kingdom. Even if you chose not to believe in fairies, that desire was still there. So why did Mum not remember?

I listened. She was quiet for a while and then, perhaps maybe because she was reading the diary, she started to cry, I could hear her through the walls and I felt terrible. I wanted to go and hug her. To say sorry for what I said; deep down though, I wanted answers too.

If I had understood Grandpa properly and I was only reading between the lines but it seemed that I was to live in the Hafan and learn enough to lead it one day. I wasn't sure how I felt about that just yet but I was pretty sure that unless Mum believed and remembered, it would be a very tough blow for her and Dad to lose me. There had to be some way to help Mum remember.

I heard her walk to the bathroom and start to run a bath; this was her escape whenever she needed time to think. I was cross with her, but at the same time, I felt bad – I had just told her that the woman who had brought her up, who she thought was dead, wasn't actually dead but very much alive and living at the bottom of our garden. Not only that, having grown up thinking her mother had lied to her, I had just informed her, in not so many words, that her mother had always told her the truth and that it was her father who had been keeping the secrets from her since Grandma Elsie had 'died'. My poor mother.

I sat for a long time, not really thinking, just staring at the walls and the ceiling and door, until I decided to get into my pyjamas and try to get some sleep. As the minutes ticked by, the feeling of regret crept closer and closer. I had the strange feeling that I was going to get a stern talk from my grandma – and that it wouldn't be as pleasant as the last time.

Chapter Fourteen
Helen

Lying in the bubbly heat of the water, I stared at the ceiling, watching the flickering patterns created by the candles surrounding the taps. What on earth was all that about? The look in Katie's eye as she had told me – it was haunting. She truly believed it and for some strange reason, it evoked emotions in me that I didn't realise I had. It couldn't be true though, I had seen my mum at the chapel, before they closed the coffin, she was definitely gone, I had kissed her pale skin goodbye and had held her cold hands one last time. There were limits – weren't there? In the subtle silence, memories of my mum and from my childhood began to flood back. Walking to school, trips to the park, shopping for dinner ingredients; the usual everyday memories of the things mothers and daughters do. But then, in the steamy heat, more memories, hazy memories that I had pushed far, far away because they could not possibly be real… I blocked them out – again.

As a teenager, I had believed myself to have gone quite mad about all the things that filled my head and my heart and I had worried about it. I hadn't told my mum. She had pushed me away with her eccentric manner – something that she had developed and used as a defence mechanism for as long as I could recall. For that reason, we hadn't been close, for at least a few years until my fifteenth birthday. Although I could always talk to Dad about anything, I couldn't always talk to him about this; he was always so technical, so logical, and the possibility of fairies living at the bottom of the garden wouldn't have worked out as a good conversation. He couldn't answer a normal question in a straightforward fashion. He would use long words and technical phrases and by the time he had finished, my mind had wandered and I never quite knew what to say in response. I knew he meant well but when a person is already panicking about their own state of mental health – it was hard to process. The questions that I needed to ask were not meant for Dad. I spoke to the only person I could. My best friend at the time, now my sister-in-law and closest adult friend, Jessica. She had never judged me, nor had she ever mentioned it since. Maybe I should phone her now, at least she had some inkling into the state of my family and my mind.

Then, I laughed out loud, mind made up. No. Definitely not. I would not talk to another person about the words of a ten-going-on-eleven-year-old. I was Katie's mother and I would figure this one out. I sighed. My mother, still meddling in my life a year after her death.

An hour later, feeling better after a bath, I checked on Katie, who was fast asleep (even though it was much too early) without a care in the world, I was sat in the armchair by the patio doors, my aching legs stretched out nestled on the footstool. I forced myself to think – about what precisely, I wasn't sure – but I knew that if there was the slightest chance to recall anything that would help Katie – and me – make sense of this nonsense, I had to try. In my mind, I trawled through what seemed like volumes of memories; the night that Katie was born – by far my biggest achievement; my wedding to Ron at the Grand Hotel just on the outskirts of town, the weather had been perfect, every girl's dream. I pushed my mind further back: my graduation; passing my driving test; my sixteenth birthday party – there had been a surprise party with a magician and I had loved every second of it! My entire family had turned up to celebrate with us; my twelfth birthday, a picnic in the garden with my friends and my first ever bike.

It was harder to focus on many memories before that. It made me tired. Like trying to read in the dark, my eyes hurt and I rubbed my temples to try and focus. The memories were dark and grainy, like an old-fashioned video that had been watched too many times and jumped, they took time to come into focus and then skipped about in my head, getting mixed up and confused. I rested my elbow on my thighs and rested my head in my hands. I started to recall something, from the depth of my mind, it was taking its time coming into focus. I fought the tiredness that threatened, I nearly had it and I closed my eyes so it could come clear.

I was restless, something was wrong. I was cross; cross that I hadn't gotten a dog for my birthday, I was ten years old and cross that everyone had looked at me when I had shouted at Mum. Okay, maybe I had been a little ungrateful – she had made me the most beautiful bag, hand stitched and it must've taken her hours: it had the most intricate design of a brilliant blue butterfly and a little girl riding on it and yet I had thrown it down in my anger at not getting the beautiful Labrador puppy that I had been gazing at in the pet shop window for weeks. I was sure they had bought her for me. The anger had turned to guilt and regret as my mum had walked out of the room, down into the garden and I had not seen her since. I knew I had upset her and I felt awful. I was watching and waiting for her across the fields. Sat between the rhododendrons and hydrangeas.

The image she had stitched on the front of the bag had been from my favourite story, the one where I was the faerie princess and I rode on a blue butterfly everywhere – he was mine and I was his. I needed to apologise…

"Evening love," the shout came as the front door clicked shut and Ron walked in, "Why are you sitting in the dark?" Darkness? What time was it? How was it so dark? Why weren't the lights on? I glanced around. "Headache?"

I was still in a daze, half awake, "Err, yes. I was just having a little sleep."

He wandered over to me kissed me on the forehead before putting his freezing cold hands on my neck. "No! Your hands are cold!"

"I am making a cold compress for you," he chuckled.

"Yeah, right. I could do with a cup of tea." I stood up and walked into the kitchen, trying to recall what I had just been dreaming about.

My birthday, my tenth birthday. I had spent most of the night sat at the bottom of the garden but I couldn't really remember why. Shaking my head, I filled and switched on the kettle. I would need to sit down and think about it, there was definitely more to that.

Part Two

The Truth

Chapter Fifteen
Elsie

There definitely was more to it than that. Sitting in the corner of the kitchen window, I had watched my daughter for the last half hour. Mulling things over, she had looked shocked, confused and hurt. I wished so much to hold her again but I couldn't – not in this form and long gone were the days when I could transition over. I had made my choice, it had been for the best. I left my human form behind two years ago.

It had been a tough but necessary decision and one that I was determined not to regret. My people, the Keepers, were of the utmost importance now; life on Earth could not and would not survive without us. Yes, it was hard work keeping the Earth but it was so very rewarding in so many ways. My one and only wish was that I could have brought my daughter with me to rejoice and revel in the beauty of it all. She had loved it as a child and I was sure, if Katie stirred enough memories, she could love it again. As it was, there was nothing I could do whilst she continued to live on in disbelief of magic, of me, of her lineage. It was imperative that she remembered.

Having royal blood in me has gifted me with many great attributes; some of which Helen and I'm sure Katie would also have inherited. I could talk to birds, insects, woodland creatures and I could understand their responses. This was another vital information source that we used to keep communications open between worlds (our worlds – there are many). We had messenger birds, dragonflies and cranes, mice and hedgehogs that could all help our messages travel far and wide. They also permitted us to ride on them without forcing and tethering them to us, there was a connection. Everything worked well together in this world. Not one creature or insect was abused for their ability or talent. Everyone and everything was appreciated for their value and worth. That is just the way it was.

There had been no great reveal of my inheritance, I had known for as long as I could recall that I had faerie blood in me. I always knew and never doubted that I would live here. Unlike Helen, you see, I was born in Hafan. I was the princess baby, born in the brightest golden buttercup, fed by the bees and butterflies, nurtured by the mice and who played with the voles. My mother was the Queen and my father the King. I lived amongst the animals and creatures of the earth until I was ten years old; at which point, my mother decided that an education would best befit us all – the world outside of ours was rapidly advancing in technology and we were not. She bestowed upon me the power, known only to a few, to transition in and out of our world and I was sent to live with a distant aunt who had chosen to live out her elderly years in human form. This allowed me to attend school and gain knowledge of languages, mathematics, science and ecology.

I surprised the teachers with my knowledge and understanding of the world and about animals and their habitats. Little did they know that I was more expert than them.

In the holidays, I became a ward of the animals and faeries who attended my mother and father; during term time, I lived with Aunt Violette. That was how I grew up to be so fluent in transition and so knowledgeable about both worlds.

However, not all was to go as mother planned. At the tender age of eighteen, I met Edward Scott at a global peace parade: it was the summer of 1968. Edward was five years older than me and had suffered a terrible blow whilst fighting for his country. He had been sent home, a wounded soldier, close to death at the age of 18 having lost half a leg in a bomb attack. Lucky to be alive, he had managed well to adjust to life over the last five years and the army had relocated him and found him a personnel job. He was a kind and loving man and we fell in love. My first summer away from home, at the age of twenty-two, was spent travelling around Scotland with him. I decided that he had my heart when he asked me to marry him. There was one problem, I couldn't lie to him. It was an agonising time, working out exactly how to tell him, yet I did – and he took it well. They say that love conquers all; well, it really did that day – with the help of a little faerie dust and a pair of rainbow-hued wings.

My mother had hoped that I would marry one of our own kind and that I would live and dwell amongst my own people, and although Edward came to the Hafan from time to time, it was soon very clear that his body and lack of faerie blood restricted his ability to live there for long. My parents worried that their only heir would be lost to them forever. However, it was my father, Rupert, who permitted me to live as a human as long as I did not forget my roots, visited twice every season and promised to ensure the continuation of our people. I made the vow-of-life, a promise that could not be broken. Even in death, the vow prohibited the soul of an anointed one from dying and they would return to the land in whatever form they were in at that time. It was therefore better for an anointed one to make good on their promise before the end of their life. I was happy, I could marry Edward and not betray my family.

The wedding was magical by both faerie and human standards; we were very much in love. I kept my promise and visited my parents every season, whilst my friends and Edwards family assumed we were taking holidays, we would be enjoying a different kind of life. We were quite the envy of our friends; 'holidays' in Wales, Ireland, Scotland and the Isle of Wight. We had our cover stories and we never faltered from them.

Over time though, the transitioning began to take its toll on Edward, it started to make him tired. Taking days for him to normalise meant that he would return to work needing time off to recover. This was not ideal and after three years, we had to find new excuses. I would 'have to' visit my mother alone, take care of my father and spend time with my aunt.

We were married for five years before our family grew. We had assumed that our genetic differences were the cause of the delay, but out of the blue, at the age of 28, we found out that I was expecting and on March 3rd, 1978, our beautiful, perfect daughter was born.

Chapter Sixteen
Elsie

Transitioning in and out of the other worlds was difficult as I got further into the pregnancy. I worried about the precious bundle inside my growing bump and so I saw my mother on fewer and fewer occasions, I missed her but I did not want to cause further complications. There was no way that I would forgive myself if anything untoward happened.

The times that I really needed my mother, more than ever, were in the first three months after Helen's birth and even though my mother could not be with me fully, I could spend time in the garden where she would sit on the pillow next to Helen and sing her to sleep, soothe her griping pains and make her laugh. It was beautiful to watch and it gave me chance to relax and sleep. Goodness knows what the neighbours thought! I recall on many occasions, the curtains twitching and I'm sure words were spoken about my inability to mother well. Through a stranger's eyes, I would leave my daughter lying on a blanket in the garden whilst I slept next to her – not exactly what you would expect a new mother to be doing.

Bringing up a child without the constant and continual support and direction of a present mother wasn't easy; I had no idea how to do some of the things I was expected to do. I would often worry – things were different in this world to my own, where the animals would care for and nurture young children (I had seen this early on in my life) so that the mother could sleep and then eventually return to her duties. Edward's parents did their best but he had been an only child, who rarely cried and had not really been ill, therefore, they were not much help to me during my times of stress. I often felt alone, even with company and if Helen cried inconsolably, it would break my heart. I had low days and high days; days where I had time to eat and sleep and days when I didn't, I praised myself if I managed to shower and didn't burden myself with worry if the dusting didn't get done. On the most part I did well, however, I had an underlying need for my mum and the rest of my family and when I was too tired, I found it near impossible to transition and see her. On these occasions, unless she was in the garden, she would not notice and I could not call her.

When Helen turned six months, I had the urge to go home, a hunger to see my parents and an urgent need. I was drawn to the bottom of the garden where I decided to try. Helen was bound tightly to my chest with a long piece of woven fabric. We did not know if Helen had inherited the capabilities to transition into our world or not and I was both nervous and apprehensive. She was such a small baby, probably because my intended height was in fact rather small, and if I transitioned and she did not, she would fall a considerable distance to the ground, who knows what harm that could cause her. So, to eliminate as many risks as possible, she was strapped to me as I lay in the soil at the bottom of the garden, between the bushes and I spoke the words, "*Yr wyf yn barod i fynd i mewn i'r Hafan.*" I clutched Helen to me and closed my eyes.

Our language derives from that of the Welsh Gwyllion Faeries who are our closest relatives. They live in the mountains of Wales and care for the rural areas of land. They are much closer to our origins, choosing not to live near urbanised areas but choosing to live in the vast outdoors. Our kind chose differently, we chose to live in close proximity of humans and to tend their gardens; we tried feverishly to keep nature alive in our own way, making a difference inner-city.

Opening first one eye and then the other, I was overjoyed to be stood in the doorway with my beautiful baby girl still sleeping and strapped to my chest. The door had swung open in readiness to greet me and I bounded through it happier than I had been in such a long time.

The scene that met me was not what I had expected. The leaves on the branches were browning and the ground underfoot was too hard – not well cultivated as I would have expected and there was a strange hush over the land, an unexplainable absence of sound. A sudden panic came over me and I started to run. I had to find my mother and father. Something wasn't right. There was no laughter, no chirping birds and the silence was eerie and uncomfortable. Running barefoot on hard ground is not easy and I opted for another option. I whistled and waited. Within just a few moments, a bright blue winged butterfly floated on the air and landed at my side; my longest friend and companion in this world, "What has happened, Auriel?"

Her melancholy whimper sent shivers down my spine. I hurriedly climbed on board and held fast as she opened her wings and took to the air. Not more than a couple of seconds later, I saw the reason and I felt the pain.

Had I realised before now, I would never have stayed away so long. My father had aged considerably whilst I had been gone, so old and frail he had become, the Keepers were preparing him for the ground. You see, when a faerie is close to death, they are committed to the ground where they can continue their existence in another way; within the plants, providing nutrition for flowers, in the sustenance the ground provides those left behind and in this way, they never truly died.

I leapt from Auriel and fell forward towards my father, "No! Don't go, let me see you first," I cried and scrambled over those who were in the way. Most people moved, others, too shocked to see their princess back again, stood rooted to the spot. The tears were flowing now and I reached out for my father's hand. "Mum, you never told me," I wept, kissing my father's forehead and holding tightly to his hand.

"You have bigger responsibilities now, Elsie," she lowered her eyes, "and we did not know if you *could* come."

I saw her shame and instantly felt love for my mother. I reached out and took her hand, placing it inside the binding that held Helen to my chest.

Until that point, Helen had been hidden from view and it had seemed that I had come alone. She gasped, "She's here?"

"Yes, Mum," I began to unwrap the now gurgling baby from my body, "everything was fine."

"You should have said you were going to try, I could have been there with you," she pondered out loud.

"I just had the urge to come here today – and now I know why… Dad?" I squeezed his hand. "Dad? I have someone to introduce you to."

He stirred ever so slightly. I picked Helen up and held her out, closer to my father, "This is your grandpa, Helen."

My father opened his eyes weakly and smiled. He lifted his hand and placed it on Helen's forehead. His eyes smiled even if his mouth did not and when he spoke, his voice was quiet and gruff, "Helen?" I nodded, "*Yr wyf yn anoint chi, Helen, i arwain ni i gyd.*"

My face fell. I couldn't breathe – I just stared, agog.

The silence in the forest deepened as my father spoke those words; a reverence and profound sacredness fell around us like a veil.

Air escaped my lips as I gasped in shock.

Eyes widened around the gathering and smiles began to appear on faces. Small faces turned to each other and eyes fell upon my daughter. Gone was the sadness, suddenly the air was filled with joy and happiness. Those important words had not been spoken in over one hundred years.

How dare he?! His last words, his last wishes annoyed me, angered me even; this was *my* daughter, and how dare anyone, even my own *father*, foretell the pathway of her life but I didn't have time to get cross at him. My father's hand fell from Helen's head and he closed his eyes, his breathing shallow, but his smile wide. Several Keepers came closer and began the ceremonious preparations for my father's committal.

I didn't move, I couldn't move; I was in shock.

Chapter Seventeen
Elsie

The words that my father spoke with his last breath were defining in our world. There was no changing the consequences. "Yr wyf yn anoint chi Helen, i arwain ni i gyd." Let me explain:

In our world, we have a royal family who govern and direct the Keepers. They ensure that the land is well cared for and producing food, that the animals are thriving and reproducing, that beauty is all around and that the world prospers from it. I am part of that royal family on my father's side. You see, the line and the crown passes from one generation to the next as you would expect, unless (and this was where fate had twisted its knife) a royal close to his last living moments, chose to pass his legacy to another.

One hundred and seventy years ago, the Queen of the Keepers, Reverie, had died suddenly; she had reigned for three short years after her elderly mother had passed her the crown. She had not married nor had she any children to pass her crown to and so it fell upon her mother (who had survived her) to take the crown once more until a suitable being was found to take on the responsibility of ruling this world.

As the elderly Queen-mother grew frailer and unhappier, a young, beautiful and kind faerieling made it her task to deliver flowers, nuts and seeds to cheer the Queen up. Each day, a different colourful treat; a new story to smile about; another day to enjoy, all because of a kind and gentle daughter of two happily married flower painters. The Queen fell quite in love with the faerieling, Lune (named after the moon) and despite her parent's rebuttal, the youngster was adopted and taken to live and learn from the Queen. In less than two years, the words were spoken. *Yr wyf yn anoint chi Lune, i arwain ni i gyd.* This beautiful being was bound to the land and the Keepers forever, and only a few months later, the elderly Queen lay down to rest in the earth.

Legend has it that Lune ruled majestically, she was kind and gentle. She cared for her people and worked amongst them unafraid of hard work and she created a happiness never seen before amongst these people. Yet, numbers were falling. There were fewer dainties than required (female keepers) to keep the birth rate higher than the death rate and Lune, after many consultations with her advisors, decided that to sustain the lifeline of her people, they must move and join families of faeries together.

It was a necessary but laborious task. First though, the birds, butterflies and bees would search near and far for a location that could sustain several generations – for the prospect of moving the access point of our world to a new location once was hard – it would be a nightmare to move again. The place had to be perfect. There had to be security and the place must provide a safe haven for anyone who chose to stay.

Many years passed and then, quite unexpectedly, a solution was found. A wonderful solution that even Lune could not have planned for.

For those young flower painters, broken-hearted at losing their only faerieling to the Queen, had left their pain behind. They had begged an old faerie-druid to take their faerie wings and make them as human as their ancestors once were. They paid for this transaction with faerie blood and their passage to the faerie world was revoked. They would never return, nor would they ever see their daughter again. The druid made sure that their life could begin immediately in a faraway town. A place where they should never have to encounter the magical world again.

As chance would have it, their love and passion for caring for the world went with them, ingrained in their very beings and this meant that their garden was truly beautiful. It was this beautiful, luscious-green garden, well known far and wide by all the flying creatures as the safest place to feed and rest; that was found by the messenger birds and butterflies. Little did she know at the time but Lune moved the access point to her kingdom right into her birth mother's garden. Surely a sign that family bonds are never broken.

Nobody really knows how it happened, only the druid was suspected to know the truth, Lune was reintroduced to her birth parents before their deaths; perfecting a way to transition in and out of her faerie being. The human couple had human children and they had children of their own. As the house was passed down through several generations, the truth behind the house and garden became lost, fairies were nothing more than tiny creatures from the storybooks of young children and the knowledge of their inheritance was lost. Perhaps that was for the best, for the fewer who knew of our world, the safer we were. Eventually, the house was sold.

My connection to this story took yet another fortunate twist; as the Queen married and had many young, the crown was passed down through the generations in the usual manner until my father was crowned King. He was a strong leader of our world and was admired for his thoughtfulness and his high regard for others.

And centuries after the old Queen's, now human, relatives ceased to live in the house, a new, young family moved in. It was from their bloodline that the handsome Edward came to exist. My Edward. It was my connection and adoration of this garden, long after I moved away to live with an elderly aunt that led me to meet him, quite unexpectedly. That was our tale.

Everyone knew the story; I knew it well. And now, my father had tied Helen's fate with the fate of the land. *Yr wyf yn anoint chi, Helen, i arwain ni i gyd* literally translates to 'I anoint you, Helen, to lead us all'. There was no going back, you couldn't alter something like this. I looked at my daughter, sleeping in my arms and didn't know whether to laugh or cry. What a future. What a life.

Chapter Eighteen
Elsie

I feel that it is important for you to know how the events of Helen's life unfolded, so here is a recount:

From that day onwards, Helen visited the Hafan every day from March to August, when the weather was warm. She would lie in the warm shade of the new spring growth of the garden and amongst the blossoms of summer, she would laugh and gurgle as the faerie babies brought her petals and pollen; as the butterflies and dragonflies floated above her, checking on her whilst I returned to my long-ago post. Petal painting. It was in my roots, in my blood and I was good at it. I would sit for hours in the garden painting daisies, their underside tips, whatever colour took my fancy, pink, red, purple. I added yellows and oranges to the petals of red roses and added depth to the simple colours of the blue bells and snowdrops. I used fine brush strokes to pick out the veins of each petal and made each flowering plant even more beautiful than it was already. I thrived on the beauty and the smell of nature. The breeze would carry Helens laughter through the forest of shrubs making me smile and laugh. I could sense that all would be well and that my daughter belonged here.

When she was one-year-old, we strapped her to the back of a ladybird and she rode through the garden, her shrieks of delight would stay with me forever. Her first word (apart from mama and papa) was 'buddafee' – butterfly – and a rather puffed up Auriel ensured that she was never far away and responded to her every gleeful gasp and less frequent whimper.

On her third birthday, my mother made it possible for Edward to transition so that he was able to spend the day with us in the Hafan. It was a magical day. Life here befitted him well and he was a favourite amongst our people. They were intrigued by his clothes and his glasses, he was certainly well looked after that day.

As she grew, we started to fear that Helen would talk about the Hafan and we decided, Edward and I, that perhaps it would be better if she didn't go as often. We didn't want her to start talking about fairies and riding on ladybirds and painting petals to everyone she met, especially once she started nursery and then school. That would not go down too well. Almost immediately, Helen became unsettled, she would cry for long periods of time, nothing could console her. Then she would wake in the middle of the night and scream in pain. We thought it would calm down; it didn't. By the fourth week, I was at a loss of what to do.

"Isn't it obvious, love?" Edward remarked one day. "Her symptoms are like that of an addict," he looked at Helen, sweating and thrashing on her bed and then he looked at me. "It is clear to me," he paused, "that the Hafan has provided some form of drug to her small body and that she is having withdrawal symptoms."

Had we known this before – and how could we have? – we would never have taken her to Hafan whilst she was so young nor would we have taken her as often. For days after this discussion, we felt a terrible guilt – yet we persisted on what we believed to be the right path for our daughter. Surely things would improve?

Things didn't calm as we had hoped, and the screaming and night terrors became a regular occurrence, continuing for months even after the memory of Hafan had seemingly left her. Then, one day, when I could cope no longer, I left her sleeping on the settee snuggled with her doll and fled to my mother. I fully intended to be back within ten minutes to check on her.

Seeing my mother and smelling the sweet fragrance of home was the tonic I needed. My nerves settled and the blood hurtling through my veins relaxed. I told my mother how I was feeling and why we had made the decision. She didn't agree fully but could see why we thought it had been best. Although she couldn't offer much advice, I felt better for having talked to her, even if I had not spent as much time with her as I would have liked.

Sneaking off to Hafan was something that I would never do again.

Ten minutes in my world, being so small in comparison, was multiplied five times in this world. The guilt I had eradicated by talking to my mother was replaced by a far guiltier feeling on my return. I had left my daughter, my helpless, unassuming daughter for fifty minutes alone in the house. I felt like the worst parent. She had been waiting for me at the bottom of the garden, clutching her rag doll when I returned, upset and forlorn. I had to lie to her because she had stopped taking about the other world and I didn't want to upset her more by reminding her. I had to sit and cradle her until she stopped crying and talking about how she had woken up all alone and scared. Possibly, the worst moment of my life.

Not many months after that, the toughness of the sleepless nights we endured helping to justify our decision, we made up our minds. It would be better for Helen if we took her back to Hafan. She would have to learn not to talk about it. I would have my mother explain to her why it was so important to keep our secret. So, about five months after we stopped her visits, Helen went back to the Hafan and the screaming and the night terrors stopped that very same day.

And so, life in Hafan continued blissfully. When Helen was five, she helped the Keepers feed the springtime bulbs so that their flowers bloomed perfectly on time, she would polish them and then she helped me to paint them once they blossomed, and as they matured through the summer months.

"It's all because of you, Mummy," she spoke out one day.

"What is?" I queried.

"All the beautiful things in people's gardens. It's all pretty because of you," she smiled, and so did I.

Edward and I pondered whether to home-school Helen or not, we didn't want her to be labelled as odd because of her mannerisms which we were sure were quite different to the others. Yet we wanted her to have friends and interact with others in this world.

By the age of six she was truly at home in the Hafan and in this world, she was settled into primary school. If she had any issues with friendships or bullying, we had resolved to remove her with immediate effect, but there had been none.

Sometimes, at the weekends, if Helen begged hard enough, my mother would permit her to stay in the Hafan without me. It was hard being home alone without her, knowing that this was how it was meant to and was going to be.

"One day, a number of years from now," I mused out loud to Edward, "we will be sat here and our daughter will be ruling in her kingdom." There was a happiness in his smile yet a profound sadness in his eyes when he responded.

There would come a time when we would have to say goodbye to our little girl. It weighted down our hearts to think about it, and whenever Helen was in the Hafan without us, we felt the tug of hard love and we struggled to deal with it.

Chapter Nineteen
Elsie

Helen excelled in school and she made many friends who would come around in the evenings to play. They were lovely girls and I was happy that they would not have a negative impact on our daughter's behaviour and attitude. Edward's job, with the armed forces, took him away from home a couple of nights a week and Helen often asked if we could stay up and talk. She wanted to know everything,

"Tell me about your life when you were growing up," she would ask. "Tell me stories about Hafan when you were living there." It was a pleasure to watch her grow into a kind and caring friend; she had a genuine interest in things, "I want to know everything I can know so that I will be good at my job."

She learnt so quickly how to keep the two worlds separate, that even I was shocked. At weekends, after her homework from school was complete, she would go to the Hafan and spend the days there, learning everything that she would need to know in order to rule and manage the kingdom. She was always popping to and fro, she found the transition so easy and could go and come back several times in the hours that she spent getting to know the place. Often she would come home asking all manner of questions; how did something particular happen? How would she know when baby bees were ready to be issued responsibility? What would happen if she made an error in judgement? I assured her that her faerie council would help with any difficult decisions and nobody would ever blame her if she made a mistake.

And so the years flew by, one minute she was six, then, in a blink of an eye and without really noticing, she was nine and so mature and well-rounded in her opinions and thought processes. Every year on her birthday, having spent the cold winter months at home (something we had decided when she was younger and less able to cope with the cold weather – Hafan was an outdoor world) we would head to the bottom of the garden together. Next year, Hafan would be ready and prepared the celebration of her tenth birthday. She would begin her life there and live here less. They would finally get their new Princess and soon to be Queen and their future would be secure once again. Life for us all was about to change dramatically.

Still, back in our day-to-day life in the real world, Helen being sent home from school ill during the second to last week of school before the Christmas holidays was not the way we had planned to end the year.

Persistent as it was, we took Helen to the doctors who said that it was probably just a winter cold, they advised lots of vitamin C and rest. When it refused to go away, we were prescribed medicines to bring her temperature down.

Helen's health got worse, she couldn't eat or drink and when we managed to give her something, she would vomit it back; after three or four days of this, we were quite concerned and took her to the local hospital emergency department. They were concerned because Helen's iron levels in her blood had dropped too low and this, they believed, was why she was so ill; her immune system was under stress. In order to treat this and because her iron count was so low, they discussed a blood transfusion. What we hadn't considered was that they would want to know everything about her diet, daily routine and lifestyle in order to identify the root of her anaemia. Although we could happily tell them most of it, we had to keep the Hafan safe. So we lied.

Helen was given a blood transfusion. The doctors explained that usually there would be a course of treatment to try and raise iron levels before a transfusion but in Helen's case, her body was in desperate need and they had no other options available to them at that time. They would need to do further tests over the next few weeks to monitor the levels and see if they could pin point why Helen's had dropped so low. After spending a couple of days in the children's ward being monitored, she regained some strength, was discharged and home for Christmas 1987.

It seemed all too obvious to us, the constant transitioning in and out of her faerie state over the years was using up her body's stores of essentials vitamins and minerals. In Edward's case, it made him fatigued, in Helen's, it made her ill. With heavy hearts, we knew that the sooner she went to live with her grandmother, the better it would be – she would not get sick once she lived there.

Chapter Twenty
Elsie

Apart from being quieter than usual, nothing seemed to have changed when Helen came home. She was eating well, watching TV, playing in her room and reading. She would ask me to read to her at bedtimes and she would sleep well and wake up ravenous in the morning. It was lovely to see the colour back in her cheeks and the smile on her face.

As Christmas approached, she became excited. She helped to choose and decorate the tree and as the presents were put underneath, she would surreptitiously shake and prod them, in eager anticipation. She did not once mention her grandmother or the Hafan in the days leading up to Christmas yet we put this down to her knowing that this would be her last Christmas with us and she wanted to enjoy it. Christmas day came and went with revelries and full bellies galore; a fun-filled family affair with Edwards parents, his brother, sister-in-law and their three children. Helen played and laughed and seemed once more to be full of the joys of life. We stopped panicking and continued with life.

In came the New Year, and January flew by; Helen was enjoying school and making more friends. February approached, came, and, as March loomed, I knew that it was time to talk to her about going to live with her grandmother. Something that I knew would be difficult to discuss, but with time approaching quicker than I wanted, there were preparations to be made and she should be involved in the decision-making.

"Helen," I broached the subject one evening as I was tucking her in for the night.

"Yes, Moma," she replied.

"How are you feeling about going to live with Grandma?"

"Grandma Scott?" she looked puzzled and for a second, so was I.

"No, my mum, in the Hafan."

She smiled and as she spoke the next words, a panic started to rise in my throat, "Oh Mum! I know that would be every girl's dream! To be a faerie princess," she giggled softly, "but you don't have to pretend anymore, I am old enough to understand now."

I was glad that the lights were out because I was sure that my face had turned scarlet and I could feel my eyes prickle with the heat of approaching tears. "Understand what, love?" I asked, my voice close to breaking.

"That they were all stories, Moma, I know now. Bedtime stories and fairy-tale. They were the best, but I know now that they were just stories."

"But –" I stopped myself from saying anything in my defence. I needed to think very carefully before I approached the subject again. This was unexpected and disastrous.

I kissed her goodnight and fled downstairs. I threw myself in Edward's arms, who could see that I was distraught and uttered the only words that I could.

"Helen doesn't believe in us anymore," I gasped for oxygen. "She has grown up and forgotten it all."

Edward looked at me. He clearly didn't know what to say. "How am I going to tell my mother? My father anointed her. She has no choice, she is the next leader of our people." I could hear my voice rising in distress. "I have to tell my mum," I stammered.

"No," Edward said firmly, "no, you don't. You can wait until her tenth birthday before you make a decision that could change anything."

And so we did. We watched her like a hawk. She didn't once go near the hedge at the bottom of the garden; she didn't once raise the topic herself; she truly had forgotten everything. We couldn't decide if it was her age and developing maturity or if it was the lack of faerie blood that flowed through her veins since the transfusion.

Her tenth birthday came and everything went wrong; we argued, she cried, I screamed and my world fell apart as I went to the bottom of the garden to speak to my mother and tell her the awful truth. The repercussions of Helen's disbelief were beyond imagination. My mother did not speak to me as I recalled the appalling manifestations that had taken place since the hospital visit and I didn't dare to visit for an entire month after she had spoken her mind. When I say 'spoken', I am putting it politely; I'm sure that every Keeper in our part of the world cowered as much as I did. The temper of a Faerie Queen is certainly much bigger than her size; it most definitely wasn't something that I wanted to experience again anytime soon.

Chapter Twenty-One
Elsie

I decided to wait until my mother sent me a sign that she was ready to talk to me. It came on a beautiful sunny morning in April when she sent a peacock butterfly carrying a crab-apple blossom into the house. It found me washing the breakfast dishes and settled on the windowsill in front of me. I stopped, shook off my hands and dried them on the towel. I offered the butterfly a dry finger and it happily took flight to meet it. It held out the petal to me and I took it with my other hand, "So she is ready to talk?"

The butterfly hovered in front of me as though beckoning me to follow.

I had thought very carefully over the past month about what I was going to say to my mother yet still had no idea. What I did know was that Helen was my daughter and regardless of the fact that she no longer believed, she was still the most important person in this equation. Not me; not my mother. We would simply have to find another way to solve the issue.

I walked slowly and hesitantly behind the butterfly, ensuring that I showed no rush to arrive at my destination. I was sure that my mother would be watching and I wanted her to see that her harsh words had pushed me away – only ever so slightly now, but at the time, far too much.

"Your offspring has ruined us!" she had spat in my face. "Thanks to you and that human man you chose, you have been the downfall of our kind." I wouldn't ever have believed that my mother could be so cruel had I not heard it for myself. She'd said, "Your father was right when he said we would have been better off with a son," had been the final straw. I had turned my back and walked away, I didn't run – part of me still hoping that there might be an apology to follow. But silence had filled our world.

I shuddered now, recalling the awful words that she had spoken. I was prepared for her to say them again, just to save myself shock. I half expected to get to the garden and not be able to get in – the final punishment. But no. I mustn't think like this – my mother had sent a peace offering. I had to accept that she had calmed down and wanted to make amends.

I stood at the door, I didn't need to speak any words for the Queen had invited and was expecting me. I felt the familiar sensation of shrinking until the door was immediately in front of me and I, the perfect height to get in. I turned the handle and walked through. The smell of the most beautifully scented spring flowers filled my nostrils before I had even stepped over the threshold. In doing so, the sight of radiant blooms were the next phenomena that met me; the pinks and lilac hues of blossom and the green, so many shades of green, shoots pricking up through the soft earth, buds ready to open and awaiting the delicate paintbrush of their Keeper to make them even more alluring to the bees and butterflies. This place, I sighed, it really was beautiful and how I had missed it. I walked on, the faerie babies came running and giggling towards me, they hugged me and sang to me, they draped me in garlands of blossoms. The animals followed close behind; the field mice and hedgehogs, butterflies and bees. It was a beautiful welcome home. Perhaps my mother had forgiven everything after all.

As I came through the trees and into the clearing, the sight before me made my palms sweaty and my heart race. What on earth was going on here? There were hundreds of thousands of fairies all gathered. Every single one of them had left their duties to gather here; for me – or so it seemed. They were all looking at me; all wearing their finest gowns and the place was decorated as if it was a wedding or a coronation or…

As my eyes met my mother's, I knew. She had found a way to overcome the gift given and wasted on Helen. I walked through the crowds, all eyes on me; mine on my mother. She was smiling and seemed calm – much calmer than the last time I saw her. She was glowing and radiant as though she had summoned all the magic that she could, so that she could perform something spectacular. When she spoke, her voice sounded like music, "Elsie, my daughter, princess of the Hafan." she beckoned me forward with a wave of her hand. Things seemed to be taking a rather serious turn here and although I was curious as to what my mother had planned, I was also terrified – not just for me but for Edward and Helen as well.

My mother looked beautiful. She wore a gown of daisy petals, delicately sewn together with the same golden thread that was used to add glorious detail to the daffodils; a crown of roses sat upon her golden hair. She was surrounded by light. As I got closer, she waved her hand at me and I felt a cold sensation run down my spine as she re-dressed me in blossoms, pink blossoms, which sashayed around my ankles as I walked. The crowd breathed in as I passed them. Something big was about to happen and I wasn't sure I was going to enjoy this. There was no turning back now though.

I met my mother and she took my hand. She created an orb around us and then she spoke to me and me alone. It was as if we were the only two fairies on earth.

"Elsie, there is no way to break the bond your father made with Helen," she paused, "but I found a way to transfer it."

I gasped, breath stuck in my throat. Hope. My beautiful daughter need not carry the unknown weight of her failings with her forever after all. Another child would, in the same way that my father's great-great grandmother had taken on an heir, my mother would do the same. A flood of relief swept over me.

"No," my mother read my mind, her face panicked, "it has to be a blood relative and, no – it cannot be me," her eyes, swollen and filled with moisture, met mine. I looked at my mother, understanding the implications, tears rolled down her face and mine.

"It was the only way, sweetheart."

"But what about my life, Mum?" I cried realising that I would be the one to leave my family to come here. My heart was breaking, "What about me? Helen cannot be without a mother, Edward will be lost without me." I fell to my knees, begging in mercy for another way yet in my heart of hearts, I knew there was no other way. My heart was breaking. I would never see my beautiful daughter again; the love of my life; I hadn't even said goodbye, they didn't' even know that I had come to Hafan today. They would never see my face again, feel my love. They would think that I had abandoned them, run away. The pain inside my chest was incomparable to anything I had ever known. I dropped to the floor and curled into a ball, my tear-stained face resting on the mossy forest floor. How could I ever be happy here now? How could I rule a world that had taken so much away from me? How could I love something that brought me so much pain?

I felt my mother sit down next to me, she laid arms on my shoulders and pulled me to her, "Elsie, my love, look at me."

I couldn't do it, I couldn't think of anything I wanted less than this. All I wanted was to see Helen and Edward and to never leave them.

"You don't understand, my sweet girl, listen to me," she lifted my face to hers and spoke clearly. "I have enlightened the spirit of your father to me and it has given me strength to continue as Queen for more years yet. You will not have to take on this responsibility for many years. Go back to Helen, go back to your husband and live a long and prosperous life. Visit me often and tell me all about my wonderful granddaughter and what she is doing. There is time yet, Elise, there is plenty of time. Live your life and when my life draws to a close, set a council in place to look after the land until you are ready to join us. Be careful in life, you must come back before it is too late – but, sweetheart, don't be sad – there is time aplenty."

I looked into my mother's eyes and understood why she was more radiant and more beautiful than ever. She had summoned the earth to give her life until I had lived mine. My heart filled with love and joy and my mother held me close to her chest. The tears of sadness turned into tears of joy as we sat inside her bubble. My vow-of-life was to come into being after all.

So, Helen grew up into a fine young lady, she met and married Ron, and a few years later, they had the most beautiful daughter Katie. The little faerie blood left in Helen's blood stream had filtered through to Katie and it seemed, from my inspection and faerie sense, that she had inherited enough of our lineage to take over from me. I had grown frail in my human form, my mother had been committed to the Earth many years prior and it was time for me to go and reside in the land I was destined for.

The faerie land took my soul and generated a new body so that my human form could be buried and mourned for. Yet I lived on, at the bottom of the garden and Edward ensured that my daughter and granddaughter moved into the house. His last promise to me.

We just had to remind Helen; otherwise removing Katie from her would be difficult.

Part Three

The Twist in the Tale

Chapter Twenty-Two
Helen

I spent a few days, mulling things over quietly in my head. Katie had not spoken about it again but I could tell that she was waiting for me to say something. I would catch her eye over the dinner table, pass her on the stairs with an air of expectation. She wanted to talk, that much was clear. She had left the diary on my bedside cabinet and it hadn't moved. Of course I had been intrigued, who wouldn't be? When Katie had said all of those things, she didn't sound as though she was telling a story; she had genuinely believed it. I had been walking around in a daze, trying not to show any emotion; trying not to let anyone see how disturbed I was. I needed to find space and seclusion to come to terms with everything and to try and make sense of it all. I needed time alone.

I got my wish the following week, I came home early from work on Friday with a rotten migraine. The minute I walked into the house, I made my way to the bedroom, climbed into bed still fully dressed and put my head under the covers. I vaguely remembered Ron coming up and kissing my forehead.

It was dusky when I woke up, the house was silent. There was a note on the pillow next to me: 'I have taken Katie to Mum and Dad's for takeaway and a sleepover. I'll be back about ten o'clock.' The digital clock blinked at me – 18:52; I needed food. I took myself down to the kitchen and switched the kettle on, pulled a mug from the draining board and grabbed a teabag from the tin. Less than a minute later, the warmth and satisfaction of a hot cup of tea was already making me feel better. I put a microwave meal from the freezer into the oven and set the timer for thirty minutes. I wandered into the living room and looked into the quietly darkening garden. Why could I not remember much of my childhood here? Why was it all blocked out by the argument with my mother? I had so many questions, the dreams, the flashbacks, the argument, my mother's stories. What on earth was I to make of all of this? No wonder I was having more and more headaches.

I put down my cup of tea. There was at least one place that I could get some answers. The diary. Katie had read it and it had made sense to her and she had spoken to my father. That was another obscurity altogether. I took the stairs two at a time, grabbed the book from the bedside table and carried it back downstairs. It was an old book, as old as me – which, for a book, is pretty ancient. I laughed inwardly at myself.

The cover was made from leather and there was a strap binding it shut. I carefully unravelled it and set it down on my knee. The pages were full of drawings, petals, blades of grass, notes, loves letters and photographs. It was a time capsule in its own right. I thumbed through the first few pages. My mother's notes whilst pregnant with me. She worried that she would not know what to do, that she would be unable to take care of me. She wrote about how her mother would have to help her. I paused at this part – I had no recollection of my grandmother. I wasn't sure if I had ever even met her. I couldn't recall ever doing so, couldn't remember going to her house; but still, there was a very vague memory of someone of stature. I shrugged it off and carried on reading.

The stories that my mother told me as a child were written in here, all of them. These, I did recall. The vibrant, colourful descriptions practically leapt out of the pages. The descriptions of animals and butterflies could easily be photographs submerged in text. There was one thing that bothered me – they were all written in first person, the way a person would recall her memories or the events of that day. Yet, there was no way that these things could be true.

The timer pinged in the kitchen and I collected the beef lasagne from the oven. I didn't really feel like eating but knew that I had to in order to stop the nausea coming back with a vengeance. But, I only managed to eat half before I thought I might be sick again so, feeling rough, took the book and myself back upstairs. This time, I dressed in my pyjamas and crawled back under the covers and into the darkness. Pulling the bin closer – just in case.

Yr wyf yn anoint chi Helen, i arwain ni i gyd. Yr wyf yn anoint chi Helen, i arwain ni i gyd. I saw an old man's face, his eyes, I looked into his eyes. I saw his past, his mother, grandmother, great grandmother. It was as if I was travelling through time. Spinning. I felt sick and dizzy.

I sat up and promptly threw up into the bin. I retched and gasped for air. I hated these migraines; they were not an often occurrence but when they struck – boy, were they bad. I took a sip of water from the glass on the table and lay back down, closing my eyes.

I was standing at a door; I was about 6, maybe 7 years old. I opened the door and walked through. Putting two fingers into my mouth I whistled. A great blue butterfly was there in moments and I climbed onto its back. I held on to the soft silkiness of its body and tucked my knees into the space crated by the fold of the wings. As soon as I was secure, she took off; I felt the wind in my hair and screamed in laughter. We landed in the clearing. I saw a lady, a very beautiful lady surrounded by light, she looked familiar and she smiled at me. "You do not know me, Helen, I am before your time." I moved closer as she continued, "Your mother called on me to help you believe." I was intrigued. Now that I looked at her more closely, I could see my mother's face.

"Are you my grandmother?" I asked hesitantly.

"I am your great-grandmother's mother, Helen, I am Lune. And I have been summoned to you, to remind you, to show you things from your past. You are needed here." She moved closer, holding out something, a scroll bound with

golden thread. "Take this, Helen. Read it; it contains your own words. Believe it, Helen."

I watched her become more distant until she was just a speck of gold light dancing high above the forest. I heard a more familiar voice, my mother's.

"It has been of great personal sacrifice to send you this message, Helen. Open your heart and mind, make the connection."

Chapter Twenty-Three
Helen

It was morning when I woke. A glorious day. I saw the sun streaming through the window curtains creating patterns on the wall. I could hear Ron in the kitchen and I could smell fresh coffee. I rolled over and felt something in the bed next to me. I sat up and moved the blankets away. I gasped and tried to move away from what I saw. There, next to my hand, was the scroll, smaller than I anticipated, that I had dreamt about, bound with golden thread. Hands shaking, I picked it up. On seeing it, I remembered writing this as a child but I couldn't recall why. It was important, I had asked my mother for some gold thread *because* it was so important.

I needed to read it but I was still weak from the night's illness and I needed coffee first. I pulled my sweater from the chair in the corner and stuffed my feet into my slippers. My nose led me downstairs to the piping hot and waiting for me, pot of coffee.

"Morning, love," Ron was cheerful this morning. "Sleep well?"

"Hmm," I nodded as I took a mouthful of coffee.

"Mum will bring Katie back after lunch, gives you a chance to relax."

"Yeah, it was a bad one," I shook my head as if willing away the memory of the pain.

"You were fast asleep when I got home, sound as a baby."

I smiled. "Fancy putting some toast in for me?" I asked with a lazy, cheeky smile on my face.

"Anything for you, Helen," he kissed my forehead and wandered over to the other side of the kitchen. "If you want me around today it's fine, just I told the boys I'd meet them for a round of golf."

"No, it's fine, you can go. I'll probably just veg for a bit then have a shower and freshen up."

"Thanks, love. I'll grab a shower whilst you eat this." He placed a plate with two slices of buttered toast in front of me, poured me another coffee and headed upstairs.

I would have plenty of time to finish reading the diary and the scroll once he had gone. I walked through to the living room and opened the patio doors. The garden looked beautiful and the birds chirped happily as they congregated at the bird table. Could there be another world out there? Was it actually possible? The laws of physics said no, but my mother and my daughter said differently and I knew more of them than I did physics. I was certainly more inclined to listen to them. It reminded me of a scene from my favourite Christmas film, if you can believe in a God that you cannot see, why can't you believe in Santa Claus – or fairies at the bottom of the garden?

Chapter Twenty-Four
Helen

I showered and dressed; choosing a light dress as the weather was warm enough for a morning in the garden and I found the garden loungers in the shed. I picked a sunny spot and set up my space for the morning, I placed a cool drink on the table alongside the book and the scroll. I was a little nervous. I picked up the diary once again and looked at the last entries, from my tenth birthday until the very last entry one week later. I had hoped that my mother might have written about why we had fallen out. I remembered that it was awful but I must have blocked out the details.

I could hear my mother's words as if she were speaking them; she was clearly distraught as her words were cold and painful to read. She spoke about how I had let the world down, how things could never be right again and that something had to be done. A little irrational perhaps but that was the way my mother was. It sounded as though there had been a plan in place that solely relied on me. But there was no actual mention of it. I thumbed back a few pages, a few months and then I read it.

August 9th, 1987, my mother had written, 'One more year and Helen will be a permanent resident.' She had planned to send me away? To live with my grandmother who I, even now, could not remember. In fact, I wasn't even sure if I would be able to pick her out of a crowd. I closed the diary. I must have said no and that must be the reason. Still a feeling nagged at me – surely there must be a memory inside me somewhere?

I decided after sitting in the warmth, just gazing at the garden for a while, that perhaps the scroll would offer more. I had indeed written it – I knew my writing and remembered the scroll; just not what was written inside it. I picked it up and looked at the intricate detailed pattern that I had drawn on; such fine lines and beautiful details. Katie had definitely inherited her art skills from me and my mother, who had also been very good at painting and drawing – especially birds and flowers and butterflies.

I was suddenly nervous. What if this scroll held secrets that my mind had deleted for a reason, what if they were painful memories, what if I had suffered something terrible and the only reason I could cope today was by repressing them? With trembling hands, the scroll sat squarely in the palm of my hand, I pulled the gold thread to untie the bow.

As it opened, I was astonished by the beautifully drawn blue butterfly – the one from my dreams. It was pale in colour and its wings even on the drawing were thin and translucent. Around the edges, there were pleats and folds and on the wings were black dots and smudges. There was so much detail: the veins running through the wings, the individual hairs on its body, the folds in the edges of the wings; that either I had been small enough to get really close and personal or (and much more likely was this option) I had studied this particular species for a very long time under a microscope and in books. The attention to detail was beyond me. How could I have been so good as a child? I could have gone on to produce pieces of art! I decided there and then to check Katie's sketchbook in case she had a hidden talent that could be nurtured unlike mine that was left to diminish.

Then there were words, tiny words; there was actually no way that I would be able to read them even with my glasses on. I squinted, trying to make out some of the words.

'To my dearest, kind and loving Mum and Dad,'

The first line was barely legible and only because it was set slightly higher than the rest of the writing. I was going to need a magnifying glass if I was going to read this! As I was sat comfortably in the sun, I rolled the tiny scroll back up and closed my eyes. It could wait.

"No! It cannot wait!" I heard the booming voice as though it had been shouted in my ear. In fact, it had been so loud that I had turned to see who was there; nobody and nothing apart from a small starling at the bottom of the garden which was looking at me – probably because I had emitted a tiny squeal in shock. I turned and without looking, reached out for the scroll that I had placed, once again, next to the diary on the table. To my utter confusion, my hand felt something cold and metallic. A magnifying glass. My mind knew before my eyes had even reached the edge of the table, but how had that gotten there?

Chapter Twenty-Five
Helen, 1987

To my dearest, kind and loving Mum and Dad,

It feels strange to be writing a goodbye letter to you when I'm not even really going away – well not far anyway. Grandma suggested that I write this because then you will have something real to hold and read. I know that I will visit you now and again and Mum, you will visit us too, I'm sure.

So really, I want to thank you for everything you have ever done for me. You gave me a happy, warm home and lots of fun. You both loved me so much and I am the person that I am today because of you. I hope that all of our memories are fond ones and that we always look back on the happiness.

My life is about to change dramatically now, so much responsibility. Grandma has her work cut out! I have to learn all the official roles as well as how to organise and plan all the day-to-day routines. I still can't get over the fact that they will trust a ten-year-old to do this – although I will have my grandma there for a while.

Today is December 3rd and I have three months until I start my official 'training' and then another year until I take over from Grandma. I am both nervous and excited. I know that I will miss you both terribly but Granddad gave me this job. I have heard the stories a million times from every Keeper of the Earth; my destiny is legend here. They have been waiting for me since Granddad was committed to the Earth and I am proud to be continuing our family in this way.

I am ready for this. It's every little girl's dream; only it's my reality.

*One day, I will make you the proudest of parents; I will be
the Queen of the Fairies.*

Do not fret or cry over me,
I will be okay;
For safe am I in the Hafan,
Where I can safely say,
I will rule with wisdom,
I will rule with grace,
And thanks to you, my mum and dad,
With love, I'll guard this place.
I will always be your daughter,
Love,
Helen xx

Chapter Twenty-Six
Helen

A wave of confusion washed over me; had I been so deluded as to believe my mother's stories? Where did I think my mother was sending me?

I closed my eyes and pressed my head into the cushioned back of the lounger. There must be more. I thought back to the argument I had with my mother, surely that would give me a clue. But there was nothing, images – but no sound, nothing helpful in any case.

A movement on my forearm forced me to open my eyes. I couldn't believe it, a butterfly had landed on my left arm. I looked closely at it – it was the same butterfly that I had drawn as a child on the letter for my parents; its translucent blue wings gently lifting up and down in the warm spring air. Was it definitely identical? I snatched the scroll out of my lap and, one-handed, opened it – using my fingers to keep it flat whilst I looked from the butterfly to the picture. It was astonishing how it looked as though the butterfly was sitting on the paper and on my arm. Down to the last black smudge it really was identical. "It's you!" I whispered.

The butterfly took flight and turned to face me.

"How can it be you? I was ten years old. Butterflies don't live that long…"

It moved a little way in front of me and then flew back, repeating this as if he was trying to convey a message.

Watching it trying with such determination to make me follow him made me more intrigued, I wanted to see if he did have something to show me. So I stood up and took a step further and another and another. The butterfly kept turning to check that I was still there. I was. Why? I wasn't sure but my curiosity was piqued. She flew to the bottom of the garden and sat on the grass next to the rhododendron bush. I knelt down next to it and curiosity involuntarily moved my finger in her direction. She sat on my finger and I felt a cold sensation come over me, I felt sick, my heart beat faster and I *finally* remembered. I remembered it *all*.

This feeling was like no other. I knew what I would see when I opened my eyes, so I didn't. All the forgotten memories flooded my brain, my senses. Everything was on overload. I would remember that shrinking sensation forever. It was cold and travelled down my spine at a painfully slow speed. It made the hairs on every surface of my body stand on end and I felt cold. I was shivering. I sat down where I was.

"Open your eyes, Helen," I recalled my mother's voice. I was a little girl again and my mother had brought me a surprise from the garden.

"No, I shan't," I had replied, with a smile on my face.

"You will love it, Helen," her voice was like song, so pure and sweet.

"Okay," I relented, expecting a beautiful flower or another brightly coloured butterfly.

Now, I opened my eyes and there, right in front of me (a now much smaller version of me) was the door. The door that I knew so well. That I had come in and out of so many times in the years leading up to my tenth birthday. I saw the familiar doorknob, the little window and the long wooden hinges that stretched the width of the door.

I knew even before the door opened what lay behind it, I had seen it all in my dreams as an adult; had lived and breathed it as a child and now, standing here, I wanted it more than I had wanted anything ever before. I felt a need and an urge to walk through the door. But it had been so long. Well over twenty years and, from everything I had read, I had not been flavour of the month when I had not returned.

No, I wasn't ready. It was not going to happen today. There were things I needed to sort first, thought processes that needed to be thought through before I started hopping in and out of another world. There was a reason I hadn't come to rule here. I sat with my back to the door, pondering the alternative.

How did I get back to being my normal human size? Although I was starting to remember everything about what lay behind that door; in that world, I was not yet ready to entertain it or revisit it – at least not just yet.

Chapter Twenty-Seven
Katie

I was helping to bath the dog in the garden when my mum called my grandparents to check that they were okay to keep me a little longer. She still didn't feel great and wanted the house with its peace and quiet to herself a little longer. It was no problem with Grandma Scott, I had been helpful all morning; I helped with the polishing, the dishes, the pegging out of the laundry and now I was half lathered up, wrestling a very wet, still full-of-suds, disgruntled dog. Mum could probably hear my wails of laughter down the phone line.

Seeing as I was too wet and soggy to go indoors, Grandma made a picnic so that I could dry off, sat on the lawn. Cheese and tomato sandwiches made with Grandad's chunky homemade bread and roast vegetable crisps. My grandparents liked to grow and make as much of their food fresh. There was a greenhouse at the bottom of their garden, raised vegetable beds and hanging tubs along the fence full of herbs. Their garden was a full on sensory experience of smells and colour and I liked it; they even made their own compost from all their household waste.

I wondered if Mum had started to read the diary yet. I had tried to get information from her for the past three days, but every time we were alone, she would find an excuse; something to do; someone to speak to; chores to instruct me to complete; any excuse not to talk to me about it. I wondered if it was the worry that I was ill or going mad that was making her ill.

I decided that I would have to speak to my grandmother again. This time without splitting myself from my body and making myself sick! I had no idea how to do it but I knew that if I could get my grandmother to invite me, the door would open and I could get access without any help from anyone else. I also had to find the perfect time when suspicions would not arise and when Mum and Dad would not worry. I started to form a plan. I would get a message to the faerie world for my grandmother and then would sneak into the garden when my parents were still asleep in the morning. I would leave a note on my bedside table telling Mum where I was just in case she came looking for me.

I was excited and also slightly nervous. This would be the first time that I would cross over of my own will. It was a big thing. This place where I had only visited once other than in my dreams was, because I had decided for myself, going to be my home. There were still a few problems to solve – my dad for one. How would we explain to him? He was certainly not one to believe in fairy-tales, he wouldn't accept me moving away and I had to go whilst I was still young enough so using the excuse of boarding school, even if he accepted that, was out of the question. I would be leaving for good. I also had to get out of school. I knew about the rules for not attending – that my parents could receive a fine – so we had to find a way to get me out of that as well!

I tried not to worry – my grandmother, with magic in her veins, would know something to help me out. She wouldn't want anyone left hurt or confused, it would all be simple when she sorted it out; of that, I was certain.

Later that afternoon once I had dried out enough in the sunshine, my grandad drove me home. "Mind you be nice and quiet when you go in, Katie. Look after your mum and tell her to get well from us too."

"I will, Grandpa." I smiled as I clambered out of the car with my overnight bag on my back.

I waved goodbye and as I turned to open the door, my mother was standing in the doorway with her arms outstretched. Instinct took me straight into her warmth and I snuggled right in as if I hadn't been hugged for a hundred years.

She hugged me hard and lifted me off the floor to kiss my forehead, "Oh, you're still damp," she mused. "Let's get you into some dry clothes and make some food, I'm starving – what do you fancy?"

"Can we do chilli tortillas with cheese on top?"

"Yes, that sounds quick and easy and fun to eat."

I raced upstairs and changed as Mum got the mince and peppers out of the fridge, the onions from their bin and a jar of tomato sauce from the cupboard. I was very good at making this meal. It was my favourite, almost as good as enchiladas – but quicker, but not as good as chilli beef calzone – that was my favourite of all, but it took much longer in the oven.

We chopped and fried and mixed, the spices were shaken in and the smell filled the kitchen. I loved cooking with my mum even if she insisted on being in charge of the frying pan (it was a gas hob and she worried that I would get burnt). When we emerged about half an hour later, we had a large bowl between us of tortilla chips, layered with chilli and then the grated cheese had been melted on top under the grill.

This was a meal to be pulled at with fingers. Dad had once tried to eat it with a fork, but soon realised that Mum and I were going to get full much quicker and he soon tossed it aside to dive in with his fingers. The room was pretty silent as we ate. I knew that Mum wanted to talk but couldn't find the words and I didn't want to start talking and take her mind off track.

Eventually, once we had eaten our fill and I was left picking the melted cheese form the edges of the bowl she spoke, "I read the diary. And something that I wrote when I was younger than you; I think I am starting to remember some things – but I don't want to see it or talk about it until I have worked out things a little better in my mind."

I nodded. I didn't have to say anything. I was already feeling much better. My grandmother would be happy with the progress.

Chapter Twenty-Eight
Katie

On Sunday morning, I woke up early, very early for me – the clock said 07:12, I dressed and wrote a note for my mum which I left it on my pillow. Thankfully, Dad wouldn't be the one to check if I was awake – he'd be instructed to go straight downstairs to make the breakfast. That was how Sundays rolled in our house. Dad would make a full English breakfast; hash browns, two types of egg, beans, sausage and fried bread, whilst Mum would make sure that I was awake, showered and dressed so that she could make the beds and gather the laundry.

Seeing as it was a bright sunny day, this was obviously going to happen. Mum had once questioned Dad if it made her strange that when she woke up on a sunny day, she would get excited about doing a wash load because she could peg it on the washing line. Dad had smirked and said something like, "Strange? No…a good wife? Yes!" and Mum had thrown a pair of socks at him in mock fury. I loved it when Mum and Dad acted childish.

Tiptoeing down the stairs with a grin on my face, I couldn't believe that I was going to try this on my own. I hadn't sent word to my grandmother but I would tell any bird or butterfly and insect that I saw in the garden to pass my message on. In our old house, there was an alarm on the downstairs doors that would have been blaring out my secret by now, but thankfully, Dad had decided not to install one here. This made my sneaking around much, much easier.

I crossed the living room and turned the key in the patio door, heart pounding in my chest. I wasn't doing anything wrong – I hadn't ever been told to stay in bed on a Sunday morning, in fact it had been known in the past for me to come downstairs early and fall asleep on the cushions, so why I was so nervous, I didn't know.

Once out in the garden, I instantly relaxed, I was drawn to the bottom of the garden, as though an invisible force was pulling me closer. The birds quietened as I passed them and even the leaves seemed to stop their swaying.

"Tell her that I'm coming." I whispered to any creature that was listening. I reached the hedge at the bottom of the garden in no time at all. I bent down below the lowest branches and found the door. I knocked twice. Surely someone would hear that. I sat down in the morning sunshine and waited for someone to come for me. I didn't know how to get there on my own, or if I could; the faerie blood running through my veins was less than my mother's and grandmother's. The further a bloodline was diluted, the more difficult it would be to connect with that world.

Helen

From the bedroom window, having heard Katie getting ready, I watched her sitting at the bottom of the garden. Although I didn't want to watch, didn't want to see what happened (just in case nothing did and Katie was upset about it), I couldn't take my eyes off her. The sunlight caught her blonde hair and made it gleam; she looked almost as though she had an angelic glow about her. It made her look even more beautiful. She kept looking under the hedge, clearly waiting; becoming more and more disappointed as time went by. I was about to go out to bring her back in when something happened to take my breath away.

Katie

I wasn't panicking; it had only been about twenty minutes and I believed. I had faith in my grandmother. I believed that she wanted to see me and that, in whatever way she chose, she would make it possible for me to see her and speak to her. I watched a butterfly go about his daily business and a bee floated from flower to flower. I admired the colours in the flowers and wondered if I would ever be able to create such beauty. I closed my eyes and listened. I heard the fluttering wings of the bees, the scratching of the birds on the grass, the wind gently blowing through the leaves; I felt the sun on my face and then I felt cold, a shiver ran down my spine, I felt light headed and a little nauseas. I was just about to open my eyes and head back to the house for something to settle my stomach when I heard it…*CLICK*.

My heart raced, the hairs on my arms and the back of neck stood on end and I opened my eyes. I expected to see the hedge and the flowers; instead, my eyes were greeted by the door. Not a small one hidden in the undergrowth. I stood up, it was a normal-sized door one that I could easily walk through. How strange! I looked around me and to my complete shock and horror, a wren was looking at me from amidst her pile of earth and twigs. Now, you may not think that that is odd, but let me explain – she was huge; she was the same size as me (and I'm four foot, two inches). It wasn't until I turned back to the door that I realised, she wasn't big at all; I was small.

The bizarre sensation that I had felt as I sat shivering in the sunlight wasn't me feeling ill, it was me shrinking. I was cold because no longer was I sat in the sunlight but underneath the hedge.

I couldn't fathom it. It was completely beyond me. Last time I hadn't shrunk, I had separated from my body, this time, there was no 'me' up there – just a small 'me' down here. I took a moment to think. I sat down again and then stood up, I walked backwards and forwards in front of the door until a voice asked, "Are you coming in or not?"

I was shocked back to sense and took the door handle in my hand and turned it. As I walked over the threshold, I gaped in awe. This was so much more beautiful than my dreams had portrayed. There were flowers and plants and shoots and sprigs of green everywhere. It was like the gardening show on television, where you come home and your garden has been transformed into paradise. Regardless of the season, every flower imaginable was here being nurtured and painted, their seeds ready for dispersal by the birds and then the insects would ensure their pollination.

I loved it already; I walked on, taking in everything – the colours, the smells, the cheerful sounds of laughter and singing. I walked through the soft grass and the tall stems of poppies and daffodils and then, standing in a clearing, no more than five feet away was the lady I had waited two years to see. She didn't look any different from the last time I had seen her and my heart melted as she smiled and held out her arms, into which I ran; my grandmother.

Chapter Twenty-Nine
Helen

One second she was sitting there and the next, she was gone. I blinked; my heart racing yet I was not worried. Any other mother would have run down the stairs in a second to get into the garden but I knew exactly where she was; she was still in exactly the same place – just smaller and that running out there would probably cause more harm than good; she was not in danger, she was perfectly safe. This confirmed to me that everything I had remembered over the past twenty-four hours was indeed real. As soon as one little bit of belief returned to me, so the floodgates had opened and so many memories had followed; helped along by my mother's diary. I was still trying to separate my adult-learnt, instinctive realism from my childhood ability to fantasise in order to keep my life normal. Everything was changing and I was tired from all the thinking. I needed and wanted to know why I had suddenly forgotten everything at the age of ten. There was only one person that I could ask; it couldn't be done over the phone and I resolved to visit my father as soon as I could. Perhaps even today, although I wanted to see what news Katie brought back. I clambered back into bed, too awake to sleep but my mind too exhausted to think clearly. Under duress, I eventually fell into a deep slumber.

I was at the bottom of the garden, my hand outstretched towards the door. I could feel the smooth, cold brass of the door handle as my fingers brushed over it. Heart pounding and mouth dry, I pushed the door. I had to duck down to get through it. Perhaps because I was now a fully grown adult, I wasn't sure. The trees and the shrubs were beautiful; so many shades of green and brown, the sea of colours that met my eyes was outstanding and the smell of each individual variety of flower and plant could be distinguished on the cool morning air. The daffodils turned to face me as though smiling at my return and insects chattered a short way away; an understanding of who I was being spread about the Hafan. It had been a long time since I had been here, especially in a knowing context. Unsure if this was a real dream or a dream-dream, I didn't care, I continued walking and enjoying.

I knew the route to take, I followed the pathway as it meandered through the flowers and long grass. I knew that after a few minutes I would reach a clearing where, no doubt, Katie and my mother would be.

It wasn't long until my memory was proven right. There was the clearing and, in the very centre, sat on an old stump of wood was my mother and next to her, Katie. They were watching me – they had not taken their eyes of me since I had arrived at the edge of the clearing and they were both smiling. The sudden urge to hug my mother was indescribable. Queen or not, rules and etiquette went out of the window as I ran to her, barefoot, my nightdress flapping out behind me, my hair a mess. I didn't care – that was my mother. I had had many dreams about this place. I had seen my mother in them. But this, this was different. This time I knew that I was here; this time I believed it. I knew that when I woke up, there would be no confusion as to my dream, there would be no worrying about what such dreams could mean.

I felt my mother's arms around me, the warmth of her breath on my forehead and I cried. I had missed this closeness. I had missed the smell of her. We had been so close once upon a time but then so distant through my teenage and adult years. We had only grown closer once Katie had been born – and now I could understand why.

"Welcome home, child," my mother whispered to me, "We have waited for so many years for you to believe in us and return. We had almost given up hope." She held me at arm's length and looked at me with such love in her eyes that

120

I forgot at once all the pain that I felt, my own eyes prick with tears as all the pain of losing my mother swept over me. I had let all my anger and frustration be buried with her and although I was worried that it might resurface, seeing my mum again over took every emotion inside me.

With a lump in my throat, I croaked, "I'm so sorry, Mum." She held me close again and I felt Katie join in the embrace. It was a beautiful moment.

Katie, sat next to her Grandmother looked so at home, she was not flustered or confused; she belonged here; just as I once did. I wanted to stay here forever but deep down I knew I wasn't actually here. I was lying in my bed with only my mind escaping to this wonderful place. I wanted so desperately to wake up, run to the bottom of the garden and live this moment for real yet I couldn't bear to leave now that I was here. We walked through the garden, talking and remembering, reconnecting and meeting new faces. The whole Royal family so to speak; the Keepers of the garden were in awe and couldn't wait to come and say hello. Older faces remembered me as a child and new faeries whizzed by on different flying creatures to get a closer look. The feel of the sunlight on my back kept me warm and the light pouring through the trees cast oddly shaped shadows on the floor. I felt content.

With a sharp jolt and a pain in my chest, I opened my eyes, back in bed; the warmth I had felt created by the sun through the window and the shadows created by Ron getting up and dressed. My heart sank and I wanted to cry; what I had missed for the last twenty-five years now burning a hole on the inside of my throat and I pulled the covers over my face to cry.

Chapter Thirty
Katie

I woke up early on Monday morning, brushed my teeth and got dressed for school. I double-checked my school bag, I had completed all my homework before dinner last night and I packed my reading book into the front pocket. Downstairs, I fought with the knots in my hair as I tried to tie it up neatly. Unfortunately, I had gone to bed with my hair still damp and it had managed to weave itself into an intricate mess overnight. Mum came into the living room from the kitchen with a cup of tea which she placed on the mantelpiece and took the brush from me. "Here," she smiled, "let me do your hair. Plaits or pigtails?"

"Plait please, Mum." I looked at her in the mirror. She looked relaxed, happy and her eyes had a shimmer to them. She looked back at me.

"What are you grinning about, Katie?"

"Nothing, Mum, I'm just happy – that's all."

"So am I, sweetheart, so am I. I will pick you up after school today." She paused, and then added quietly, "Dad's working late." Her voice faltered ever so slightly with nerves. The intonation in her voice was clear – we would have time to talk without Dad being in the house. An indescribable feeling of excitement welled up inside my chest, Mum and I now shared the secret, no more was it just me living a double life, keeping secrets, it was both of us; we knew more about this world than most other people and we knew it together.

I liked school. I loved learning and practising skills. Yet today, I could not wait for the day to be over. My maths lesson seemed to last forever, assembly was boring, playtime was cold and long and English just didn't inspire me like usual. I ate my packed lunch in the dining hall without talking to anyone and even when my friends sat down with me, I had nothing to say. I smiled and nodded at their jokes without paying much attention. They must've noticed that I wasn't myself because I overheard one of them say, "She might not be feeling well." The afternoon wasn't much better. PE and geography weren't my favourite lessons on a good day so today, when I wanted things to be over quickly, they were even worse.

The bell finally went at half past three and once dismissed, I grabbed my coat, bag and lunch box and was out of the school gates in no time at all. Mum was waiting and within minutes we were on our way home.

There were no words spoken, I could tell by Mum's demeanour that she had had the same kind of day as me. A 'couldn't-wait-for-it-to-be-over' kind of a day. I threw my bag on the sofa, next to Mum's handbag and watched her go to the patio doors, unlock them and throw the doors open.

"Dad has a dinner meeting with work and he won't be back until eight o'clock," she spoke without looking at me. The time now was 3:48; we had plenty of time.

For anyone looking out of their window, they would have seen a mother and daughter walk to the bottom of the garden, kneel in the grass and look at the flowers in the hedgerow. Nothing unusual. Except in the blink of an eye, they disappeared and the onlooker would question whether they saw anything at all.

"*Yr wyf yn barod i fynd i mewn i'r Hafan,*" Mum spoke.

I looked at her puzzled, she smiled back and held her hand out, I clasped it tight and felt the strange cool sensation running down my spine. I counted to ten inside my head and when I opened my eyes, I was stood outside the small wooden door, with my mum standing next to me.

"How did you know what to say?"

"I remembered – I used to come here all the time. It just sort of – came back to me."

"It was pretty awesome," I grinned.

"It was, wasn't it!" she laughed.

I turned the door handle and pushed the door open. Mum's face was a strange colour. I took her hand and together we walked through the door, it closed behind us. Mum was trembling now.

"Don't be afraid, Mum," I whispered, "This is where we belong – this is our home."

She looked at me, a tear forming in her eyes, "It's more beautiful than I remember."

"You were only here last night, Mum, I was puzzled."

"That was a dream; this is real. This is very real and very different. I can actually smell the flowers."

She walked on, looking around her, stroking flowers, touching the grass; admiring it all. She watched the insects buzz around and gasped when her mother's butterfly came close. Auriel had been a part of the family for centuries; she had enjoyed an extraordinarily long life for a butterfly. Suddenly, as if under instruction, all the butterflies, dragonflies, ladybirds and bees were escorting us through the forest. We stepped over logs and ducked beneath low boughs and around flowering plants, their buds bursting and ready to bloom.

Helen

Spending an evening in the presence of my mother was the most amazing experience. All the feelings of loss and the pain of losing her had subsided in moments. Feeling her skin on mine as she stroked my face and seeing her tears fall, erased all the discord between us. Years of angst and guilt vanished in that moment.

That had been four hours ago. Once the light started to fade, Katie and I had come back to the house although neither of us had wanted to. We hadn't spoken much, just wandered aimlessly through the house and up to bed. The intake of information and the sensory overload had worn us both out.

There was only one worry in the back of my mind, constantly niggling, circling me around and around and always bringing me back to the same point. It was all well and good Katie and I knowing what the future held; how on earth were we going to break this to Ron? This was something that I would need to think carefully about, perhaps talk to my mother again. There must be some kind of faerie magic that would smooth things a little.

Before I drifted off to sleep, I called for my great grandmother to help me and she did not disappoint. There most certainly was something spectacular about the faerie world. However, the words that she spoke and the knowledge that she passed on to me, were both unexpected and unbelievable.

Who would have thought that Ron, my open and honest husband of many, many years would have been such a secret keeper? Who could have predicted the tale that he had to tell.

Chapter Thirty-One
Ron

I love my family very much. Helen had stolen my heart the moment I saw her, and her parents, Ted and Elsie, were the best in-laws a guy could have hoped for. I knew of them before I met them, though not through the usual and most likely connections – but I will come to that later.

I knew Elsie had a big secret and I knew that Helen didn't buy it. They didn't get on as well as Elsie would have liked and although the animosity between them had dispelled over the years, it didn't fully dispersed until Katie was born. Ah, my beautiful daughter Katie who had inherited her mother and grandmother's magical blood – as well as a little something from me. Helen, having not accepted her bloodline, was oblivious to her daughter's birth-right – yet I was quite aware of it – it had been quite obvious to me for quite some time and I had sensed it even before she was born.

To look at her, Katie had the bluest eyes, the most golden hair and the rosiest cheeks. For most children, these colours fade and change throughout the early years of their life – yet for Katie, she was like an exquisitely painted doll and these colours had never faded. Her personality was just as beautiful. She saw the splendour in everything and her grandmother's heart lifted when she saw her. She sensed it as well as I; the small babe that Helen cradled lovingly in her arms would be the answer to all the uncertainty. She was the solution to all the problems that mattered.

But, already, I can hear your confusion. How did I know about the magic? How could I sense it? Well that is quite a tale to tell.

Part Four

Revelations

Chapter Thirty-Two
Ron

I was not at a work's dinner the night that Helen and Katie went to visit the Queen of the Keepers. I had learnt of their plotting in a way that only a father and husband could, you see, men listen more than people give them credit for and the subtle changes in a wife and daughter's body language can give away so much; usually this is covertly noticed when a surprise party or a secret gift is being discussed in secret. So, it was inevitable that I had discovered their secret meeting and discussion and I was not far away at all, watching the story unravel from my vantage point.

But first, let me explain. Let me tell you *my* tale.

Over a century ago, my people (another tribe of magical beings) had to leave their ways and their magic behind to integrate back into society – this was not entirely by choice. It was essential. Having lived a quiet life for such a long time, we had begun to die out, as fewer and fewer second and third generations were born to us. There was only one community of us and unlike the Keepers, we were unable to relocate and regroup to ensure our numbers survived. It was for that reason that we happened into everyday society and we used what little magic we had left to cover our tracks, and to assist those around us, to believe that we had always been there, a concrete part of their everyday lives and memories.

Before I had left my mother, father and brother to be integrated into human society, my family (or what was left of them) lived in the trees. Our presence and our magic nurtured them yet that was not our intended purpose – just an additional bonus that we could use to our advantage. We, the Elkin-folk, ensured that the levels of natural resources provided to earth were maintained. The natural gases in the ground, the oils and minerals found in the Earth's foundations, that allowed a balance between the layers of earth were kept perfectly in order, thanks to us. If one mineral was lacking, we would create an environment perfect for regeneration. In doing so, we ensured that every plant with roots was kept healthy. This pleased us. Unlike the faeries, we hadn't transformed from human form, we always existed just as we were. Ever important. Every being had a role, the youngest of our kind – and the eldest (those too young to and those unable to burrow deep down into the earth) would help to maintain the quality and integrity of plant leaves and their ability to absorb carbon dioxide. The more we harnessed these nutrients, the healthier the plant became and the more we could use the nutrition as they passed through the plant and the roots.

In a way, like many of the small magical beings that humans are unaware of, we were once the sole reason that life on the planet survived. The world has its own circle of life amongst plants and magical beings. The root of the trees would send signals to other tribes in charge of the weather and rain or sunshine would be accommodated as necessary. It was all very simple. Whatever the world needed, magical beings would ensure.

The intricate world of magic cannot be fully imagined or described in words, too many varieties exist and too few know the full extent of them. Humans are completely oblivious to the amount of magic that exists in their world. They comment about 'coincidence' or 'luck' without ever truly understanding the truth behind these things.

Often, when a human thinks that they have had the most wonderful idea, it is because they have overheard a faerie discussing such things – for magical folk are far more creative than humans. Such is true as far as tales of magical and mythical beasts go, the ones that humans have never seen but have heard of – unicorns are a prime example. The unicorn is indeed a real creature, with the look of a horse, glistening white with a long, silver mane and tail, a rainbow-hued horn on their forehead and the magical ability to increase life expectancy. However, it exists in our world, not the human one. It supports the life of all magical beings allowing them to survive for many years. No human will ever see one even though they encounter them daily. Unicorns are as small as particles of dust and are in the very air that humans breathe, often seen as shiny specks dancing in the sunlight.

One very famous faerie tried to explain how the magical world is linked to the human one, it isn't quite right, but it's close. Insomuch as it is not true that a faerie dies every time a human confesses their disbelief, it is true that when humans take their world for granted, when they use all of the Earth's natural resources to feed their greed and line their pockets, the magical beings have to work harder to maintain and sustain the world. This leads to exhaustion and eventually the inability to function properly. So it was true, that over the years, as more and more natural resources were mined from below Earth's surface, more work was created for the Elkin-folk to maintain natures balance.

It was in the early 1900s that one of our leaders decided that the natural resources within the earth could no longer be sustained. It was near impossible to replace everything that the humans were mining and the balance, being so important in regeneration, was almost lost completely. Percival, a rather intelligent Elkin had a ground-breaking idea that some of the things that humans had created using natural resources could be reused instead of mined. It was his decision to leave our realm in order to establish this idea in the human world. If it worked, it would allow us time to regain the earth's natural sustainability.

And so, we were given time once again over another century to co-exist with humans in a world that was beginning to regenerate, thanks to recycling and a new care and respect for planet earth.

Due to the sheer amount of magic that exists on Earth, most magical communities are unknown to each other, so well-disguised and hidden they are. I was lucky though. My father before me was a being full of intrigue and, inquisitive in his nature, he often asked questions or delved into things that others would simply accept as 'truth'. He desired knowledge, for after all – knowledge is power and my father liked to think of himself as quite powerful.

It was my father, during one of his 'meddlesome' explorations, in his younger years, who discovered the 'painting lady' – a faerie who was sat basking in the sunshine, taking so much care in her painting as she dipped her brush and coloured the daisy's petal tips the most glorious shade of pink. From then on, so taken in by her beauty, he would often hover close by and listen in on her conversations with the others of her kind. He did not always understand them as the older beings would speak in a different tongue, but the younger ones, they were full of excitement and would often regale their tales loud enough for anyone who wanted to listen in.

It was in this manner that my father learnt all about the faerie princess. She was excited and animated and ever so beautiful. Having had no contact with other magical beings, he became obsessed and fascinated with watching her and he used every opportunity to learn as much as he could about this new species. He visited the garden several times over the years, each time learning more about the magical beings. He watched the faerie princess grow and eavesdropped on her gossips and conversations with the other faeries, he heard about her betrothal and her plans to be wed and then about the beauty of their wedding day and the soon arrival of the first royal baby. He felt her joy knowing that he himself would soon become a father, and once I was born, he told me all the wild and wonderful stories of a faerie princess who lived in her kingdom, not too far away.

He filled my head with tales of wonder from a young age and by the time I was old enough to venture away from our tree, there was only one place that I wanted to go. Unfortunately, there was not the opportunity for me to see the princess; the one occasion that I visited the garden, the young princess had gone to school in the human world and by the time she came home, our world was in so much turmoil that I was preparing to leave my home and my parents, forever.

I was ten 'human' years old when I integrated myself into my childhood home with my 'mother' and 'father' (although I had lived more than ten years in my world, I was about the same size and stature of a ten-year-old boy). My new parents were a middle-aged couple – late 40s, who had been unsuccessful in bringing their own children into the world due to a medical anomaly that years of tests had been unable to reveal. Still, they were very close and very much in love with each other. Being the sole reason for each other's survival, they had very little contact with other, more distant family members and it was easy for me to weave a magical web around them; giving them fond memories linking their past to me. It wasn't cruel to force myself on them as I am sure you are thinking, I was giving them everything that they had ever craved, plus, having magic around them did more than weave my existence into their life; it provided an element of healing so great that they had indeed gone on to have their own child. A boy the very next year. A beautiful little brother for me and the long-awaited (albeit unknown – as my magic had erased their pain and sorrow) son and heir. He was so tiny and the feeling of love between us all emanated for miles. Each smile brought warmth and happiness immeasurable. It was perfect, I wasn't jealous of my new baby brother like some children are when they become less 'important', I was, instead, the proudest and most caring and generous big brother that anyone could ever wish for. I was part of a loving family and I, along with George, received the best upbringing that any being could have cherry-picked for themselves.

Chapter Thirty-Three
Ron

So, back to the present day. Long gone were my magic capabilities. Unlike my father, I was unable to sit in a tree and listen to my wife and daughter's chit-chat. I was instead sitting just inside the garden shed as they sat, cozied around the fire-pit, discussing me and their recent discovery. Helen had explained the message from her grandmother to Katie and she hadn't yet spoken any words. I was as eager to hear her speak just as I'm sure Helen was.

"So…" she began after what seemed like an age, "My magic didn't just come from you?"

Of all the things that she could have started with, the lies, confusion, questions, she wanted to link her magic not just to her mother – but to me as well. I loved my daughter even more right now and my heart swelled with pride.

"I hadn't thought of it like that, sweetheart – but, I suppose it does."

"And does it mean that I am heir to two magical kingdoms?"

Again, I was stumped. Was my daughter not in the least bit concerned about why I had kept the truth from her for her entire life?

"I really don't have the answers that you need, darling," soothed my wife.

How I wished for just a drop of magic to feel their emotions and read their minds right in that moment. I wanted to know that my wife did not have feelings of angst towards me and that my daughter still loved me. I needn't have worried. Katie spoke up, "I guess we just need to ask him then

– it must have been very hard for him to keep such a big secret from us –" she paused, "Maybe he didn't know – like you?"

"Your great-grandma suggested that he knew and that it had torn him up inside for years. She said, that wondering if you were magic and whether I would remember my own lineage, had been playing on his mind for a number of years."

"Well then, that's sorted – we'll just tell him that we know and then we can make a decision on what to do next. There is no point in us worrying about what he will think of us – especially if he has known all along!" she laughed the most beautiful laugh and Helen joined in.

"You are the most wonderfully understanding daughter," I could almost hear her smile, "and we are very lucky to have you in our lives."

I couldn't agree more and for the next hour I sat in the shed and listened to them talk about my past through the stories Helen's great grandmother and Katie's great-great grandmother had told. I could share these with you now, but I'd prefer to tell them to you another time. You could say that it was a little bit magical.

Chapter Thirty-Four
Katie

The next few days, weeks and months passed in a happy blur of smiles, summer holidays and a new family secret which we all shared. Instead of what could have been a bitter and painful experience of sharing secrets and lies, everything had gone smoothly. Mum and Dad talked for hours into the night most nights and I darted forwards and backwards from Hafan and home learning my role and preparing my move there. I chose my new nest (a horse chestnut shell that was so soft and lined with nature's silk that I could easily fall asleep in seconds once cocooned in there) and I met my faeries in waiting. It was a little peculiar at first, to be waited on – but as people often jest, I would get used to it! I had my own chariot and my own butterfly to transport me around Hafan.

Back in the human world, I got the distinct feeling that Mum and Dad loved each other more now than the day that they had married. When they looked at each other, their eyes went all glassy and Mum would blush. One evening, as I watched, I remember thinking that they were like two lovesick teenagers and I think the little magic left in their blood took years off them as they settled down together on the sofa to watch some slushy lovey-dovey film. It was nice. The house was full of happiness and love and laughter. It really was a lovely place to be.

There was never any ill exchange about the secrets of the past, after all it was and had been there on both sides of the family and because no one had spoken openly about it for centuries, there seemed little point in discussing it now.

The evening after Mum and I had discussed the revelation, we talked to Dad about it. He told us that he had overheard us and was glad that it was all out in the open. From then on, he would tell us about his childhood and his parents, the life that he had enjoyed before moving into the human world. I promised never to reveal his secret to my grandparents; they did not need to know and would not be able to comprehend the tales and magic of it all. They were still and always would be my grandparents – regardless of the difference in our genetic makeup.

Dad shared his hope that one day I would be able to find someone else from his lineage and that connections could be made for the first time between the two magical worlds. It was a nice thought, but we had no idea where to start. It was a thought to be shelved until such a time that we had some clue on where to begin. I think deep down he missed his family and the life that he once had. He had blocked it out for so many years and now that he was able to discuss it, he was clearly homesick. Mum could understand to a point but she was also able to visit her world as it had not been completely destroyed.

The only niggling thought inside me (and it was a mixture of both excitement and nerves) was my final move – the day that I would say goodbye to my life as I knew it. Of course I could return when I wanted, but for the most part, my duties and responsibilities in the Hafan would take so much of my time that Mum and my grandmother refused to set anything in stone. Firstly, I had to finish this year at school, I would be removed for 'home-schooling' and I would move to Hafan forever. I would be able to visit Mum and Dad who would remain living in the house but I knew that they would continue to grow older (and much quicker than me) whilst I would remain young for many years and possibly centuries to come.

The words nervous and excited didn't even touch the surface. But I knew that not only was this move essential, it was right and it was what I wanted.

I would spend my time being taught under the guidance of my grandmother and her faeries. Oh what a whole new world this would be. I would learn about the importance of our role in the grand cycle of the Earth and I would eventually rule once my grandmother passed to the ground. There was a lot to take in and sometimes the idea of the responsibility scared me. Still, I knew that this is what I wanted and deep down I knew that Hafan was the place where I belonged. Whenever I visited, I felt it in my blood. It's the way you feel when you arrive home after a hard day at work, exhausted and aching and you finally get to sit in your favourite armchair where all those feelings dissipate and you relax.

And that was why, on September 1st of the following year, when I should have been going to high school, I was instead walking down to the bottom of the garden with no belongings – what would I need with them? – except a locket that Mum and Dad had given me. Inside was a picture of me sitting in between them both, big grins on all our faces after a fun day at the beach.

Mum and Dad were happier than I had ever known them and they had always been happy. There was a glow about them that could only radiate from happy people. The faerie blood in me meant that I could see it literally shining out of them. I was proud to be carrying on the work of my grandmother and I knew that I would be coming back in a few months' time – I mean, Mum and Dad didn't know yet – it was a privilege only to those with a great deal of faerie blood in them but there was another secret. This time, it was one that I was keeping from them. I knew something that would ensure their happiness endured for years to come, Mum would find out sooner or later and Dad would be so thrilled. I would definitely be coming back within the next twelve months, I mean, any big sister would want to meet her new baby brother – wouldn't she?

Epilogue

A memoir to end with.

Having had the chance to spend some time with my parents and grandparents over the last ten years has allowed me to document this history. It is rare that one faerie life can be documented in both the human and magical world. I became Queen of this world within a year of my transition and it was my grandmother who placed my crown on my head. Mum, Dad and my brother Sephan (my father's father's name) were able to enjoy the celebrations which were held in the garden.

Since the passing of my parents; from natural causes after a shorter than average – but still a very full and healthy life, (I believe that magical blood wanes when away from its true home) my brother and I inherited the house. Sephan knows all about our family tree and has accepted it willingly. He has turned twenty-five and although he has never been through the gates of Hafan, he and I have met often in the garden to talk. We are very close and very similar yet it was his decision to stay in the human world. He lives in the house and it is pleasant to see him from afar every day.

I was married within five years of moving to Hafan and my grandmother passed into the Earth shortly afterwards. I had learnt all there was to learn from her before she left and she had fulfilled her promise to her people and the time was right.

Theodore and I are very happy and have three faerielings to keep us busy. Rose, Summer and Ronald are all very energetic and are a daily reminder to us of the precious gift of life.

The Hafan continues to provide safety to all magical creatures yet we still await contact from any beings from my father's bloodline.

It has been a pleasure to be a part of the writing of this memoir and I hope that it serves as a reminder to my grandmother's bloodline in the human world of Hafan and all its good work and intentions.

It is on this note that I leave you with love, always.

Katie
Xx